DUSTY AYRES AND HIS BATTLE BIRDS:
THE GREEN THUNDERBOLT

THE GREEN
THUNDERBOLT

By Robert Sidney Bowen

ALTUS PRESS • 2017

CHAPTER 1
EXPLOSION PATROL

TAKING A sip of his tall drink, Curly Brooks riffled the deck of cards impatiently, and nodded at the four other H.S. Group 7 pilots seated about the mess lounge table.

"Snap into it, suckers," he grunted. "There's two bucks of my dough in that pot. How many cards?"

Dusty Ayres, on Curly's right, thumbed his cards, selected two and tossed the others away.

"Three of the best," he said. "And I don't care if they're all aces."

"Sorry," grinned the other, dealing him three. "I'm using aces. Next?"

The next two shook their heads and tossed in their hands. But the fourth, Red Colgan to the gang, after considerable frowning deliberation, took two.

"And none for the dealer," chuckled Curly as he laid the remainder of the pack on the table. "I play these, and one buck says they're good!"

"Your buck and up one," Dusty came right back, shoving the money to the center of the table.

Red Colgan frowned some more, then snorted and threw his hand down.

"Out!" he growled. "Damned if I'll go on supporting you two tramps forever!"

Curly shot Dusty a keen side glance.

"You wouldn't try to bluff papa, would you?" he muttered. Then with a shrug, "Oke, there's my buck. Beat a straight, queen high?"

For an answer Dusty laid three aces and a pair of jacks on the table.

"What do you think, sweetheart?" he grinned. "And thanks for those aces. You did give them to me!"

Brooks glared at the hand, and heaved a sigh.

"Talk about luck?" he growled. "No wonder the Blacks never pin you for keeps!"

"Luck?" chided Dusty. "My boy, that's science—science and skill!"

A burning retort on Brooks' lips never came off, for at that moment a field orderly came into the room and clicked his heels in front of Dusty.

"Major Drake's compliments, skipper," he said. "He wants you in the Group office at once."

"Right," nodded Dusty, raking in his winnings. "Coming on the jump."

Curly Brooks tilted back on the hind legs of his chair and gestured hopelessly.

"See?" he addressed the others. "That's the life of a hero for you! Never gets a moment to himself. Always tearing off to get another medal hung on him. But does he wear them? Naw! He's saving them to hock in his old age. Oh well, at least the game will be honest, now!"

Dusty grinned and as he walked around in back of Curly's

chair he hooked a toe on one of the legs, and jerked. Brooks let out a howl, fanned air frantically to regain his balance but crashed over in a sprawling heap.

"Oh, I'm so sorry!" mimicked Dusty from the door. "Are you hurt? I hope so!"

"You bowlegged bum!" roared Curly scrambling to his feet and hurling a seat cushion. "I'll fix you!"

But with a thumb to the nose salute, Dusty dodged outside and let the cushion smack harmlessly against the closed door. With Curly's bellowing voice still ringing in his ears, he walked swiftly over to the Group office and shouldered inside.

"Present and accounted for, major," he said, saluting the big officer seated back of the desk. "Something special?"

The C.O. shrugged, and slid a square of paper across the desk.

"Your guess is as good as mine?" he grunted. "Just came over the radio from Washington H.Q."

Dusty picked up the paper and glanced at the short message.

Major Drake,
C.O. H.S.G. 7.

Captain Ayres is herewith ordered to report to Test Field No. 12 at the earliest opportunity. If in air, signal down at once.

Bradley,
Chief of U.S.A.F.
Washington, D.C.

"Report to Test Field Twelve?" frowned Dusty, switching his eyes to the major's face. "What the hell?"

The C.O. gestured blankly.

"Search me," he replied. "I'm only a Group commander, so why should Washington H.Q. take me into their confidence? Better get going at once. You can make it in a couple of hours, easy. Major Trapp is C.O. of Test Twelve."

WITH A nod and a salute, Dusty went outside and over to the hangar line. A flight sergeant saw him coming and yelled to a couple of mechanics to dolly the Silver Flash III out onto the tarmac.

Two minutes later Dusty sent the trim ship streaking down the take-off runway and zoomed it up into a cloudless sky. At the top of the zoom he shortened the climb angle, but continued on up to twenty thousand.

Leveling off, he set the ship on a dead-on course for Test Field 12, turned on robot control and slouched back against the headrest. Pulling the order from his tunic pocket he read it again, and found the words to be exactly the same.

Lips pursed, brows furrowed in thought, he drummed his fingers against the cockpit side.

"Wonder what it could possibly be?" he grunted aloud.

As though expecting to find the answer to the unusual order, he stared fixedly at the instrument board in front of him. Suddenly, he realized that the red signal light on the radio panel was blinking rapidly. Slipping the phones over his head, he snapped on the set and spun the wave-length dial.

"Captain Ayres of the...."

He cut the rest off with a curse, and quickly shoved the phones off his ears. For a moment he thought that both his ear-drums had been broken. The instant he'd spun the wave-length dial knob the phones had blasted shrill, staccato sound. It was like the peak pitch of a police siren—like a thousand people whistling for a dog. So loud and penetrating had the noise been that it made the inside of his head ring like a four-alarm fire.

But as the ringing died away, he turned down reception volume, and gingerly eased one of the phones back onto his ear. The whistling was still quite loud. But as he listened to it, he suddenly realized that it ceased at intervals, and that during the pauses the ear-phones crackled with the dot dash of the secret Black Invader high speed wireless code.

For nearly ten minutes he listened to the high speed signals. And during that time he tried every wave-length reading registered on the dial. Every one was blocked with the weird sound. Then, like the shutting of a sound proof door, the whistling stopped abruptly. The red signal light on the radio panel winked out, and the ear-phones gave forth nothing but silence.

Hesitating but a moment, he shot out his hand and spun the wave-length dial knob to the Washington H.Q. reading.

"Captain Ayres calling Washington H.Q." he said into the transmitter tube.

And then the light winked, and the phones crackled the "on your wave" signal.

"Reporting strange static jamming and enemy code signals

on all wave-length readings! Sending direction unknown. Directional finder did not register. Did you pick them up?"

"Yes," replied the ear-phones. "But we haven't been able to check yet. Waiting for reports from key directional finder stations now."

"Signing off," called Dusty. "Just wondered if you heard them. So long!"

Snapping up the switch, he stared out past the glistening nose of the Flash toward the haze-covered southern horizon. Then impulsively he switched his gaze to the radio wave-length directional finder on the dash.

"Damn funny, you didn't register!" he murmured at the instrument. "Somehow I'd like to know where that came from. Oh well, I guess Washington can find out."

DISMISSING THE incident from his mind, he turned off robot control, took the stick and nosed the Flash down in a long, slanting dive. Eventually Test Field 12, located a few miles south of Wichita, hove up over the horizon lip.

Twenty minutes later, he slid in to a gentle landing right smack on the tarmac apron of the row of five big cement and steel girdered hangars. As he legged out, a field sergeant ran up and saluted. There was a mile-wide grin on the non-com's face.

"Don't often see landings like that one, skipper," he said. "Mind if I look her over, sir? We've heard plenty about this crate."

Dusty returned the grin and nodded.

"Help yourself, sergeant. As a matter of fact, you might fuel her up. Where do I find Major Trapp?"

The non-com pointed a grease-smeared finger toward a low stone building at the far end of the hangar line.

"In there, skipper, with them two big bugs that flew in from Washington this morning. Been a lot of secret doings around here during these last few days!"

Dusty hunched his shoulders.

"I don't know what they're all about, sergeant." Then over his shoulder, "Don't fuel her too much. She throws a bit at times."

"O.K."

Walking swiftly down the tarmac and over to the stone building, Dusty paused long enough to rap his knuckles on the heavy wooden door, and then stepped inside. As he entered, he checked a gasp of surprise, clicked his heels and saluted smartly.

In the room were three officers. Seated behind a big oak desk was a short, heavy-set man, whom Dusty guessed at once to be Major Trapp, C.O. of the field. On Trapp's left was General Bradley, chief of Air Force Staff. And on the other side, sat none other than General Horner, chief of U.S. Intelligence.

It was General Horner who got up and came forward to greet him.

"Glad to see you, Ayres," he smiled. "Didn't expect you so soon. Oh, yes, this is Major Trapp. And of course you know General Bradley."

Dusty nodded, saluted the two men again, and stood waiting expectantly. There was a moment of silence, and then Major Trapp took charge of things.

"Have a chair, captain," he said, motioning with his hand.

And after Dusty had seated himself, "By the way, feeling fit after that last mix-up of yours?"

"Why—why sure!" the pilot blurted out. "Never felt better in my life." Then giving them all a sharp questioning look, "This isn't another medical board, is it?"

"No, not this time," laughed General Horner. "But it so happens, that we've a damnable job for you. It's a job for one pilot in a million. That's why we've decided to give you first chance to volunteer. I want you to hear the facts, though, before you decide anything."

Pausing, the Intelligence chief turned to Bradley.

"Suppose you acquaint Captain Ayres with those details, general," he suggested. "It comes under the flying division of your department."

The chief of Air Force Staff nodded, picked up a pencil from the desk and toyed with it absently as he fixed deep-set eyes on Dusty.

"The first part of what I have to say to you, captain," he began presently, "you probably know quite well. However, I wish to begin at the beginning so that you will get the entire picture.

"Shortly before the outbreak of the war, when we first realized that a Black invasion was inevitable, Air Force Staff succeeded in getting the Congressional Committee to appropriate a sum of several millions for the establishment of the Technical Air Research division. As you of course know, out of that division came the original design for your own plane, the Barling XFB, and several other advanced weapons of war.

"However, unknown to all but a select few, the division has

been experimenting for some time on what is called the X-Ray-oscope. It's a telescopic arrangement that enables the human eye to penetrate fog, clouds or smoke and view objects clearly at a distance of two hundred miles. Even the dark is no obstacle to the X-Rayoscope."

The general paused—for emphasis, Dusty thought.

"The experiments have been completed!" the senior officer continued. "The X-Rayoscope is a success. Now, though it could be used to good advantage in ground work—by our troops, I mean—it was decided that the Air Force should give it its first practical test.

"Naturally, we insisted upon that, as the instrument was a development of the Air Research division. However, because of its weight, some nine hundred and twenty pounds, it was necessary to design and construct a special plane suitable for stratosphere flying."

The senior officer paused long enough to nod his head at the C.O. of Test Field 12.

"Under the supervision of Major Trapp," he said, "such a plane was executed. Actual tests gave it a ceiling of almost eighty-five thousand feet. With the X-Rayoscope aboard, the ceiling should not be more than three thousand feet lower."

The chief of Air Force Staff stopped talking for the third time. But this time, Dusty felt that the other two men became tense and leaned forward.

"I've been speaking in the singular," spoke up the general with startling suddenness. "My error. I should have said that two X-Rayoscope units were constructed, and two of the specially designed stratosphere planes were built. Now, last evening, preparations were completed for the first practical test—a test to be conducted over enemy territory.

"Captain Carter, Major Pratt's chief test pilot took off in plane Number One. He sent down radio reports of his progress all the way up to eighty-two thousand feet. And for an hour after that he contacted us at intervals of five minutes. His last report stated that he was slightly south of Detroit and able to see clearly every detail of the Black defenses between Lake Huron and Lake Ontario."

"His last report?" echoed Dusty, as the general made another one of his tantalizing pauses. "You mean—"

"I mean that we never heard from him again," the other finished quietly.

Dusty misconstrued the expression of bitter sadness that came into Bradley's face.

"Force landed, and the Blacks got the ship, eh?" he murmured.

"NO. HE was destroyed in the air," replied the general. "Bits of wreckage, that we have positively identified as coming from his plane, have been picked up as far south as Toledo. And, according to a report from the commanding officer of the Detroit area, at about the time Captain Carter stopped radio communication there was a terrific explosion high up in the air. As it was night and the Detroit area was swathed in clouds, no one saw the explosion."

Unconsciously, Dusty looked at Major Trapp. The test field C.O. saw the question in his eyes and shook his head.

"No, it couldn't possibly have been the plane, Ayres," he said firmly. "To save weight we loaded the ship with just enough fuel for an hour's flight at top ceiling. Carter was going to glide in for a landing."

"The X-Rayoscope," said Dusty, turning back to General Bradley. "Anything in it that could have exploded, sir?"

The Air Force chief shook his head emphatically.

"Nothing. I wondered myself, and checked with Air Research, but they declared that there wasn't a single part of it that could possibly explode!"

"Nor could it have been a Black plane crashing into Carter," muttered Major Trapp, as though speaking to himself. "If the Blacks have got a ship that can reach the altitude Carter was flying at, I'll eat it!"

Silence settled about the room for a few moments as each mulled over his own thoughts. Presently Dusty looked up at General Horner.

"When do you want me to test the other ship, sir?" he asked quietly.

Horner half smiled, then frowned.

"Wait until you hear the rest of the story, Ayres," he said gruffly. "We're not suggesting that you do a thing—yet!"

"I'm waiting, sir," replied Dusty evenly.

"It's not much," began the other. "And perhaps it has no connection at all with what General Bradley has just been telling. However, I can't help but feel that the two link up in some way.

"Late yesterday afternoon, one of my best agents got through to me direct on the radio-teletype machine. I thought he was working back of the Black line in Canada, but the message he sent through was code-dated Texas. And it read—Here, read it yourself."

The officer fished in his pocket and handed Dusty a sheet of paper with typing on it.

15—X-34—T-6
Warn all air depots T-6—M-9… stop…. Blacks at Mex-12
have new—destroy—areas—D-4 first—seven—will—

Dusty puzzled over it for several minutes, then raised questioning eyes to General Horner.

"I get the part about warning all Air Force depots from Texas Six to Michigan Nine, sir," he said slowly. "But the rest has me guessing. Mex-Twelve is Chihuahua, Mexico, isn't it?"

"And D-Four is Detroit," nodded the Intelligence chief. "That's just the way the thing came through. I tried to check back to fill in those blank spots. But I was unable to find any answer. Something must have happened to the agent."

Dusty, who had been studying the queer message again, suddenly straightened up.

"Detroit Four?" he echoed looking straight at General Bradley. "What time was that explosion over Detroit last night?"

"Figured you'd get that," spoke up Horner. "From reports, it happened at exactly five of seven, and about three miles south of the Detroit Air Concentration Base. I—"

Horner stopped abruptly as the desk phone jangled. Major Trapp answered, then handed the instrument to General Bradley.

"For you, sir. Washington H.Q."

The Air Force Staff chief nodded, put the receiver to his ear and bent over the mouthpiece.

"Bradley talking! Yes, Williams? What? Repeat that!... My God, no! When.... Well, order all assistance possible, Williams! The whole area must be evacuated at once. I'll check back with you later."

As the man hung up, his eyes were large and slightly glassy. His face was chalky, and little beads of sweat were oozing out on his forehead. For nearly five seconds he stared fixedly at the opposite wall. Then he spoke.

"The Dayton Air Base was completely wiped out by a terrific explosion twenty minutes ago. Not a man survived!"

CHAPTER 2
PHANTOM DEATH

THE OTHER three men received the startling announcement in stunned silence. Like stone images they sat motionless, eyes glued on Bradley's face. It was Dusty who snapped himself out first.

"How, sir?" he demanded. "What happened? A bomber raid?"

The other shook his head.

"According to Williams, my aide, no one seems to know. There's no one alive to tell. Everything within five miles of the base was razed. By God—that means that there's nothing left of that special high speed bombing Group in training there. They were to lead the Vermont offensive next week."

The general suddenly got to his feet and swept them all with an apologetic glance.

"You gentlemen will have to excuse me," he said. "I must get the Dayton area at once. I'll leave the other matter in your hands, Horner. Excuse me."

Before any of the others had time to rise, the Air Force Staff chief had turned on his heel, and was going through the door. As it closed Horner cursed softly and pounded a fist on the desk.

"By God, that proves it!" he boomed. "I am right. The two things do connect up. First Detroit, and now Dayton!"

"You mean—" began Dusty.

Horner cut him off with a curt motion, leaned forward and tapped a thick forefinger on the garbled teletype message.

"I mean that this is our one clue!" he said sharply. "Agent Fifteen found out that the Blacks were doing something in Mex-Twelve—something that had to do with what happened at Detroit and Dayton. He tried to contact me with the details, and—well, something happened to him."

"You really think that there are Blacks in Mexico?" Major Trapp asked.

The general shrugged.

"It's possible. And this message makes me believe it's a fact. Hell, we all know that a couple of armies could hole up in the Chihuahua hills and never even be noticed. Didn't Pancho Villa do it years ago?"

"But the Mexican government," Trapp started to protest, "is—"

"Is in the middle of another one of their confounded revolutions!" Horner finished savagely. "One half of the population doesn't even know what the other half is doing. The Blacks are aware of that, and while they've been keeping our main forces busy on the Duluth-Bangor front, they could easily have slipped into northern Mexico. That's what they did, blast their hides!"

"But where would that get them?" argued Trapp. "Our Southwestern army would smash them to bits if they tried to cross the Rio Grande. And granted that some of them succeeded in slipping past our Pacific fleet patrol, they certainly couldn't land enough guns and equipment to be of any danger!"

"I disagree, sir," spoke up Dusty. "I think I get General Horner's meaning. The Blacks originally landed most of their troops by air transport in Canada. They could do the same thing in respect to Mexico."

"Exactly!" nodded Horner vigorously. "And right now they are trying to wipe out our Central States air defense depots, and—unless I miss my guess—force us to draw in Pacific and Atlantic coast units to fill the gap."

"But how?" questioned Dusty, frowning. "No bomber raid could have wiped out Dayton that way."

Horner gestured hopelessly, and looked Dusty straight in the eye.

"That's why I suggested that General Bradley call you down here, Ayres," he said quietly. "If anyone can answer that question for us, you can."

"You mean you want me to reconnoiter Mex-Twelve with this X-Rayoscope?" the pilot asked.

"I do. A ground patrol in the Chihuahua hills would be futile. And a regular air patrol would be sighted too far in advance. But with this X-Rayoscope you can hang up over the Texas border and give us a detailed report on the entire area. From your report we can decide whether or not to contact the present Mexican government and send troops across the Rio Grande."

"That won't be difficult," said Dusty easily. "But there's a question I'd like to ask."

"Fire away, Ayres. We've got a couple of hours to wait 'til dark, anyway."

"IT'S ABOUT that," said Dusty, nodding at the teletype message. "You said you thought Agent Fifteen was in Canada, but it's code-dated Texas Six. How do you know that this Agent Fifteen really sent it through? Couldn't it be a trick of the Blacks to draw our attention away from some other point? Mex-Twelve is a long, long ways from Detroit and Dayton, sir."

"I know," replied Horner. "But, it couldn't be a Black trick. They know that Agent Fifteen is dead. They caught and killed him a month ago."

"Huh? But—"

"Wait 'til I finish. Agent Fifteen died one month ago. But, one of my other agents, whose number and identity are known to the Blacks, arranged with me to use the number fifteen when he wanted no one but myself to know who was reporting. The idea is to checkmate any Black attempts to use his number on fake messages. In short, any message that comes through from Agent Fifteen, is genuine."

Dusty leaned forward muscles tensed.

17

"And he is really Ag—"

"Exactly!" General Horner shut him up with a fierce look of warning. "That's why I put so much faith in this message!"

Dusty wanted to kick himself for almost speaking out of turn. Horner had shut him up so that he wouldn't blab out the truth in front of Major Trapp. The truth that Agent 15 was really his pal of a thousand wild adventures—Agent 10, General Horner's son.

Dusty stared at the message in silence. What had happened to Jack Horner? Why had he garbled the last of message? And why hadn't he answered the general's check-back?

But there was no answer forthcoming. Nothing but the concrete knowledge that Agent 10 had sent through a warning. Perhaps it had been the final dying act of a brave man. Or, perhaps—But the fact remained that the torch had been flung down, and it was up to him to carry on.

Raising his eyes to Horner's, Dusty nodded slowly.

"I understand perfectly, sir," he said in a low voice. "And with your permission, I'll get started pronto. Where is this X-Ray-oscope plane?"

Horner didn't answer. Or rather, for an answer he looked at Major Trapp. The test field C.O. started to ask a question, but instead shrugged and stood up.

"At a small field forty miles south of here," he said. "We can all go in my car."

In silence the other two stood up and followed him outside and over to the field motor transport park. Getting in behind the wheel of a grey, low-slung, stream-lined job, Pratt motioned them in back, and kicked the starter. A minute later they were swinging onto a dirt-packed road that ribboned off across the country side in a southerly direction.

Settling back against the cushions, Dusty glanced at General Horner. The man was riding with eyes closed, so the pilot refrained from asking the dozen odd tantalizing questions that were racing through his head. It was doubtful if the Intelligence chief could answer them anyway. He'd been given all the available facts. From now on, he'd have to find out the answers himself.

But, as he stared dully at the seemingly endless strip of road ahead, he wondered if there were any answers to the crazy mix-up. Supposing he did find out that there were Blacks in the Chihuahua hills? What would that prove relative to the reported explosion high over Detroit, and the terrible destruction of the Dayton Air Base?

Yet, Agent 10 had said to warn all air depots from Texas Six to Michigan Nine. In other words, from El Paso to Detroit. Warn them against what? Bomber raids? Ridiculous! The Dayton ground detector units would have picked up bomber engines long before they arrived. And—

He suddenly stiffened as he remembered the crazy whistling sounds and the Black Invader high speed code signals that he heard on the way to Test Field Twelve. Was it possible that that had been the Blacks' method of blanketing out raiding bomber engines?

But, even as he asked himself the question, he unconsciously shook his head. Static-jamming wouldn't blanket out engine sounds to ground detector units. And besides, the whistling sound couldn't possibly have been meant to do that. If it was, why were the Blacks sending out code during the intervals?

A WILD shout from Major Trapp at the wheel, and a sudden furious burst of speed, snapped Dusty out of his cockeyed reverie. Trapp was hanging onto the wheel with one hand and pointing excitedly ahead with the other.

"Something's happened!" the words came whipping back. "See that smoke? That's from the field where the plane is! God—it must be!"

Following the direction of the officer's hand, Dusty saw a cloud of oil-black smoke oozing skyward about ten or fifteen miles ahead. Often he had seen that same kind of smoke during a sky battle, and he knew instantly that it came from burning fuel and oil.

Grabbing the back of the front seat, he braced himself as Trapp fed maximum hop to the thirty-two cylinders and sent the car streaking along the narrow dirt road. Beside him, Horner did the same thing, and above the roar of the engine, Dusty could hear the Intelligence chief cursing bitterly to himself.

Suddenly he was almost thrown into Horner's lap as Trapp slammed on the brakes, skidded the car off onto a side road, and then sent it racing forward again. Sun-baked shrub growth flew past the windows. The road ahead leaped at them and flashed by underneath the wheels. A dozen times Dusty steeled himself for a crash, but each time Trapp avoided disaster by a hair's breadth.

And then finally, the car shot around a wooded bend in the

BLOOD-FILMED EYES STARED AT HIM.

road and careened toward a small field less than five hundred yards ahead.

At the far end of the clearing stood a small hangar which looked as though it was a made-over barn. From the rear half flame and smoke belched upward. And through the open front door Dusty was able to make out the smoke-blurred outline of a short, barrel-fuselaged, low-winged monoplane.

He lost sight of it as Trapp slammed on the brakes and almost threw him into the windshield. Rubber screamed, and the car spun around in its own length before it finally mushed to a full stop. Out jumped Trapp, bellowing like a madman.

"Where the hell are they?" he roared, as he started running. "Damn their souls, I told them to stand—"

Dusty didn't hear the rest. He was too busy pounding ground toward the flaming hangar. He and Trapp reached it shoulder to shoulder, and without checking speed they dashed inside.

Trapp stumbled over something, flung out his hands for support, and grabbed only thin air. He went sprawling on his face. Skidding around, Dusty bent down to give him a hand. It was then that he saw the crumpled figure of an American soldier on the hangar floor. The man was quite dead, but blood still trickled out from a small, blue-black hole in the middle of his forehead.

"God! What happened?"

Like a man suddenly paralyzed, Major Trapp crouched on hands and knees, staring wide-eyed at the dead man. Dusty didn't bother to answer him. Like a flash of light, he smashed his open hand against Trapp's face.

"Give me a hand with this plane!" he thundered.

As he spoke, he jerked the officer up onto his feet. Trapp stared at him glassily for a second then gulped.

"Right! Thanks! Come on!"

Bodies bent over low, they plunged into the swirling smoke. Choking and gasping Dusty managed to get a dolly under the tail of the ship. Then yelling to Trapp to take hold of the handle with him, he swung the tail around and began tugging the ship out through the open door. By now, General Horner had puffed up, and with his help they finally pulled the ship into the clear.

The instant it was free of the hangar, Dusty dropped his hold on the dolly handle and raced back into the now blazing inferno. He practically fell over the dead soldier before he found him in the smoke-filled barn. Bending over, he scooped the dead man into his arms and staggered outside.

"Others!" he gasped at Trapp. "Any others?"

The question seemed to snap Trapp out of his trance. He stiffened, nodded jerkily.

"God, yes! A sergeant—Sergeant Caldwell!"

DUSTY WHIRLED, and suddenly stopped short. Then he veered off toward a blood-smeared figure in regulation OD trying to crawl around the corner of the hangar. Bounding over to him, Dusty grabbed his arm and dragged him clear of flames.

"Thanks, sir—no use. Got me—lung!"

"Don't talk, sergeant!" Dusty commanded, as he tried to make the man as comfortable as possible. "Just take it easy."

Blood-filmed eyes stared at him. Then they switched to Major Trapp, who had rushed over, and flickered with recognition.

"Sorry, sir—some one set fire—oil drums back of hangar. Shot Bolton! Got me—when I ran out."

"Who did, sergeant?" asked Trapp as he bent over the man. The non-com shook his head weakly.

"Don't know. Didn't see—just got shot—"

The rest trailed off to a gurgling moan. Then with a sharp gasp the man arched his back, dug blood-caked fingers into the dirt, and collapsed. So he died.

Slowly, Dusty got to his feet. Then without a glance at the others he turned and walked over to the plane. To all outward appearances the fire had not damaged it. But as he jerked open the cabin door and started to climb in, he stopped short and groaned.

The interior of the cabin was a mass of crumpled and broken metal and glass. A large tripod mounted, cannon-shaped instrument had been broken in a dozen places. The forward end, which originally extended through a specially constructed channel in the instrument board, had been hammered free. And the instrument board itself was a splintered, twisted slab of wreckage.

Dusty turned to call Trapp and Horner. They were standing right back of him, bitter defeat stamped on their faces. It was Trapp who spoke first, and his voice seemed to come from the bottom of his boots.

"Wrecked! They wrecked it—the only other one we had. It'll take a week—at least. And in the meantime—"

He left the rest hanging in mid-air, as though reluctant to finish. Horner suddenly pushed past him, stuck his head inside the cabin and looked around. Eventually satisfied that his eyes did not lie, he straightened up, and stared grimly off into space.

"Licked us again!" he grated harshly. "God, if I could only get my hands on the damn agents who did this! God—now what?"

On impulse Dusty reached out and touched him on the arm.

"Just this, sir!" he said sharply. "We're not licked. Now, we go to work!"

General Horner stared at him dully.

"Too late," he grunted thickly. "With this you might have seen something. But now—"

"Now, I'm damn sure I'm going!" Dusty cut in. "General Horner, I'm asking you for two things. One, permission to use Test Field Twelve radio. Second, a free hand for forty-eight hours!"

The Intelligence chief gave him a long, searching look. Then presently he sucked in his breath and nodded.

"All right, granted! Knowing you, I won't ask your plans. But—what's Test Field Twelve radio got to do with it?"

Dusty grinned.

"A lot, sir. As things have turned out, I've a hunch this is going to be a two-man job. So, I'm going to radio Lieutenant Brooks, of my gang, to join me. You know of him, I believe, sir?"

"Yes, I certainly do!" Horner grunted. "Another crazy sky Indian—thank God!"

CHAPTER 3
STRATOSPHERE MISSION

S NUBBING OUT his cigarette, Dusty leaned back and nodded at Curly Brooks seated beside him in the mess lounge of Test Field 12.

"And that's the whole picture, kid," he said. "Maybe we'll only draw a blank, but we've got to have a damn good look-see at the Mex-Twelve area. Acting as protection for each other, I think we'll be able to do the job O.K."

Brooks said nothing as Dusty finished. For an hour he had been listening to his pal and General Horner tell the story from the very beginning. Major Trapp had gone back to the other field to salvage what he could of the X-Rayoscope unit.

"Well, kid," spoke up Dusty again, as Brooks didn't speak. "How's it listen to you?"

"Like a fairy tale," Curly grunted. "But if you think a look-see will help, then its oke with me. Always did hanker to see Mexico from the air."

General Horner frowned and leaned forward.

"I wouldn't take it too lightly, lieutenant," he snapped. "Frankly, I don't feel particularly good about letting you two go. Perhaps it might be better to fly a Group patrol."

"Can't agree to that, sir," cut in Dusty. "If there is something funny going on around Mex-Twelve, a Group patrol would be too much of an advanced warning. But with just Brooks and myself—well, maybe we could be a couple of lost pilots taking the wrong way home.

26

"Now, here's my plan of action. Curly and I will arrange to be at maximum altitude, south of Mex-Twelve, at dawn—exact. Then down we'll go, hedge-hop every square mile of the area, and smoke for Texas Six. What we do after that depends upon what we see. However, I'm going to try and pick up your son's trail at Texas Six, and find him, if I can."

General Horner's eyes dimmed a bit. He started to speak but checked himself abruptly, as there came a sharp rap on the door. A signal lieutenant stepped inside. He went over to Dusty and held out a message form.

"Here's a reply to that H.Q. request, skipper," he said. "Just came through."

"Huh, what's that?" Horner asked, staring at Dusty. "H.Q. request? For what?"

Dusty didn't bother to answer. He took the message and glanced at it eagerly.

Captain Ayres
c/o Test Field 12.

Re: inquiry. Cross check of key directional finder stations place static noise and code signals somewhere in southwestern area. Oscillation in reception volume indicates signals sent out by aircraft gaining altitude. Signals heard 4:20 P.M. to 4:30 P.M. Again from 6:15 P.M. to 6:20 P.M.

Faber

Washington H.Q.
Radio Base.

A thoughtful light creeping into his eyes, Dusty handed the form to General Horner.

"Checked on those queer sounds I was telling you about, sir," he explained. "Note the last. Signals heard again from six-fifteen to six-twenty!"

The Intelligence chief stared at the message again, then raised questioning eyes.

"Well, what about it?" he demanded.

Dusty shrugged.

"Not sure just what," he replied. "But somehow it seems to me that it fits into the cockeyed mystery, somewhere. According to my figuring, from what General Bradley told us, the Dayton Air Base was wiped out at just about half past six."

Horner gulped and nodded.

"By God, that's so! Good heavens, the more I try to untangle the damn mess, the more mixed-up it becomes."

"Same here," agreed Dusty, getting up. "So, I'm going to stop figuring, and do something instead. Come on, Curly, let's check the ships and get underway."

WITH A grunt, Brooks heaved himself up and followed Dusty outside. In silence they walked over to the hangar line, where the Flash and Curly's ship were waiting. Parting, they spent the next half hour checking their charges. Then they joined each other for a last minute cigarette.

"It all sounds screwy, if you ask me," muttered Brooks as he held the match for his pal. "How the hell can anybody at Mex-Twelve do anything about Dayton Air Base?"

Dusty puffed in silence a moment.

"That's what we're going to try and find out," he murmured. "I agree with you, it sounds screwy enough. Except for one thing, I'd chuck the job right here and now, and agree to a Group patrol."

"And that one thing, is?"

"That message from Jack Horner," Dusty replied. "He doesn't go off half cocked. He got a-hold of something big—and something happened to him before he could get clear details through to his father. Mex-Twelve or no Mex-Twelve, you and I, kid, are going to find him!"

"Jake with me," grinned Curly. "A great guy, Jack Horner. I only hope—"

He left the rest hanging in the air.

"So do I!" said Dusty through clenched teeth. "O.K., let's go. Remember, wing to wing up to maximum altitude. Fly without lights, and keep an eye on me for signals. No radio stuff, unless you have to. Never can tell who might be listening in."

"Right!" nodded the other turning toward his plane. "See you over Mexico for breakfast!"

Five minutes later Dusty got the takeoff signal from the field control tower, and sent the Silver Flash thundering down light-flooded runway. Swinging up in an easy arc he throttled a bit and waited for Curly's blue ship to claw air beside him. Then wing to wing they both climbed through the night-darkened skies.

At thirty-five thousand, Dusty leveled off and set the nose of the Flash dead-on for Mex-12 area. Throttling so that Curly would have no trouble in keeping pace with him, he slumped back in the seat and stared ahead. He tried to analyze all of his myriad thoughts but the result was merely a hodgepodge of sensations, the strongest of which was the premonition that invisible danger flew with him.

Just why the feeling stuck he couldn't explain, even to himself. Inwardly he had scoffed at General Horner's fears for their lone patrol over Mex-12. He'd automatically considered the flight as good as done, plus the fact that most of his concern was centered about finding Agent 10.

But now, as he raced across Oklahoma and Texas, a strange foreboding of impending disaster rippled through him. He tried to dismiss it with a curse, but that didn't help. Without realizing it, he caught himself repeatedly searching the darkness ahead, as though he expected to see some weird and fantastic doom come charging out of the night.

Then, as though fate were actually justifying his jumpy nerves, something weird and fantastic did come charging out of the night. It came from high above him—an egg-shaped blur of pale green light that slammed down past, in front of him, at terrific speed. So fast did it travel that his eyes had no sooner become focused upon it than the thing was lost to view in a cloud layer far below.

It was just a flash impression of green light shaped like a falling drop of glowing rain water. Though his brain had automatically calculated that the thing had passed him about half a mile away, his plane went skidding upward, and the interior of his sealed cabin felt like the inside of a blast furnace. For one hellish moment he thought that the plane was in flames. But gradually the cabin air cooled down to normal temperature.

Hauling the craft back onto its course again, he turned in the seat and stared out at Brooks' plane. But he saw nothing but a dark sky with a faint gray streak of light low on the eastern horizon. Pulling back to half throttle he banked around in a wide circle, frantically searching for the moving shadow that would be Curly's ship. But it was to no avail.

FINALLY, DUSTY took a chance, spun the wave-length dial knob to Curly's reading and grabbed up the transmitter tube.

"Curly!" he called. "Have lost contact with you. Flash wing lights for a couple of seconds, so I can pick you up."

As he spoke he leaned forward and swept the darkness with his eyes. But not one single flash of light did he see. Three times he repeated the request. But each time the result was the same—nothing.

"Can't spot you, Curly!" he finally shouted. "Call me back on your set, at once!"

But he might just as well have been talking to a stone wall. The signal light on the radio panel didn't wink once. Little icy fingers began to clutch at his heart, and slamming on full throttle he thundered about in ever widening circles.

"Damn that guy's hide, where the hell, did he go?" he shouted at himself. "If—"

He never finished the rest. At that moment the cloud layer far below became fused in a great sea of yellow and red light. For perhaps four seconds Dusty stared down in blank amazement. Then the light died out and total darkness closed in once more.

About half a minute later, the Silver Flash trembled violently from prop to tail wheel. It was as though it had suddenly rushed into the spiraling vortex of a raging tornado. Before Dusty had time to check it, the plane whirled around in two complete turns of a flat spin, and then went skidding out on wing-tip.

Cursing, he slammed it back on even keel, spun the wavelength dial to S.O.S. Emergency and grabbed the transmitter tube again.

"Calling Texas ground stations!" he yelled. "Saw the glare of an explosion at approximate map position T-Four. What happened?"

For several seconds the signal light stayed dead. Then it blinked and a harsh voice crackled in the phones—a voice that Dusty recognized immediately. It was the Black Hawk!

"I'm afraid that the ground stations are too occupied to answer you, captain. So let me tell you. There was a very splendid air base at map position T-Four, but it exists no longer. Unfortunately it met the same fate as your Dayton Base, earlier this evening!"

Too stunned for the moment to even think of any reply, Dusty sat staring at the radio panel. Then with a savage curse he shook himself out of his trance.

"Damn your soul!" he roared into the transmitter tube. "What the devil do you mean? And—and where are you?"

"I mean exactly what I said!" came back the grating, chuckling answer. "And—look below you, captain!"

Unconsciously, Dusty leaned forward and looked out below him. A split second later he was slamming the stick over against the cockpit side and hurling the Flash into a vicious half-roll.

"Dummy!" he snarled as singing steel came hammering down from above. "Didn't you know any better than to fall for that one?"

Boiling with rage at being caught by such a simple, stupid trick, he skidded out of the roll. He jerked the nose up in a screaming zoom toward a shadowy blur that was spitting twin streams of flame across the skies. Jabbing home both trigger trips he returned the "compliment" and grunted with savage satisfaction as the other ceased firing. Then the shadow went darting away.

"First crack, and you muff, eh?" he roared into the transmitter tube. "Well, now have some yourself—and see how you like it!"

A grating laugh answered him, and before he could close up the gap for a cold meat shot, the Hawk's plane slapped into a dive and went racing earthward. Virtually pounding the trigger trips, Dusty went racing down after him. But the Black's quick dive gave him a lead, and it was next to impossible to make a long-range hit in the darkness.

Nevertheless, Dusty clung doggedly to the fleeing target and kept both his guns ripping out slugs full blast. Eventually, the Hawk's plane tore into the cloud layer and became lost for good. It was then that sane reason took charge of Dusty once more.

Killing his "waste" fire, he eased the Flash out of its wild dive and went zooming upward.

"Sorry, captain," the ear-phones suddenly crackled, "I have something else more important to do. Perhaps at another time—after you have completed your little secret patrol!"

The last crashed against Dusty's brain like a salvo of gunfire.

"He knows! My God!"

His own muttered words made him come to. Steeling himself, he coolly took stock of the situation. It all summed up to one thing—the plan to look-see the Mex-12 area had been knocked higher than a kite. The Black Hawk, himself, knew of what Dusty intended to do. Hell, he hadn't thought that that rat would be within two thousand miles of him. Yet, they had just met—over Texas.

HE SUDDENLY thought of Curly Brooks. In the last few hectic minutes he'd completely forgotten his pal. What had happened to Curly? Had the Hawk downed him? No. He would have heard the gunfire. Yet—and that explosion too! Had Texas-Four air base been destroyed? The Hawk had said so.

He suddenly let out a curse, and smashed a clenched fist against the side of the cockpit.

"Hold it, kid!" he growled at himself. "One thing at a time!"

Steadying his nerves, he let the Flash loaf through the air at half throttle, and tried to make up his mind as to his next move. Should he return to Test Field 12, or should he go ahead with the look-see patrol over the Mex-12 area? The two questions burned through his brain.

But before he could make any decision, the red signal light

HE RETURNED THE COMPLIMENT...

on the radio panel blinked and the voice of Curly Brooks in the ear-phones sent his heart leaping.

"Calling Ayres on Five-Seven-Eight. Radio dead for last ten minutes. Check back on my signals!"

Dusty's hand flew to the transmitter tube. He opened his mouth to speak, then snapped it shut and shook his head.

"Wait a minute, stupid!" he grated softly to himself. "Don't go telling the world everything you know."

Then as Curly Brooks repeated his request, Dusty suddenly made up his mind.

"Signals received!" he called into the transmitter tube. "Company arrived. Fly destination and contact as arranged. Signing off!"

Snapping up the contact switch he checked his position and once again set a dead-on course for Mex-12 area. As he went tearing southwestward, he dully tried to reason out just why he had decided to go on with the original patrol. Was it because Curly had turned up, and he believed that somehow the two of them would manage to muddle through? Or was it because he'd met the Hawk, and wanted to be one up on the Black?

"No, it's not that," he murmured. "It's because that rat, knowing I'll be there, will be there himself. Meeting him way down here, kid, means you're close to something big."

A little over an hour later, he was swinging around in lazy circles, at maximum altitude, over the southern edge of the Mex-12 area. The light of dawn was slowly driving the night shadows westward. Already, he could see the top fringes of great cloud banks drifting slowly below on their unending travels.

Inwardly, he thanked the gods for putting those clouds there at just the right time. At least the men on the ground wouldn't see him. Of course, if Blacks were down there with ground sound detector units—then that was something different.

Right now the question was—where the hell was Curly. The sky was getting light fast, and he hadn't spotted his pal. A few moments later, as he swung around to the west, he caught a glimpse of the blue ship sweeping up out of the ground-blanketing cloud banks.

Automatically, he poked the nose of the Flash down and joined his pal. Across the air space he saw Curly's lean face grinning at him. He grinned back, raised his free hand and pointed down. Curly nodded in reply, and his blue ship tilted earthward.

Dusty started to shove his own stick forward, when suddenly the signal light on the radio panel blinked rapidly. He shot a frowning glance at the wave-length dial, suddenly realized that some station was calling him on S.O.S. Emergency wave. A moment's hesitation and he snapped on the wave-length contact switch. Out of the corner of his eye he saw Curly level off and reach a hand toward his own radio panel.

"On wave-length!" he called. "Go ahead!"

"El Paso relaying emergency call to Captain Ayres!" replied the ear-phones. "Identity and plans known. Return to original base at once. Message signed, X-Thirty-four."

The El Paso station repeated the message three times, and then signed off. Cursing softly, Dusty sat glaring at his radio panel. X-34 was General Horner, and he was recalling him because in some way the Intelligence chief had discovered that his identity and plans were known. Well, that was no news. But—

He left the rest of the thought unfinished as Curly came swinging in close. The lean pilot was shaking his head vigorously, and a few seconds later his voice crackled in Dusty's phones.

"What the hell, we didn't come just for the ride! Let's see it through, anyway!"

"Damn tooting!" Dusty yelled back. "Props down!"

With face grimly set and eyes narrowed, he sent the Silver Flash streaking down toward the drifting cloud banks.

CHAPTER 4
THE SILVER FLASH

IN THE last few seconds before the cloud mushed up to engulf him, Dusty shot a snap glance back over his shoulder and made sure that Curly was hugging him close.

"Now, we'll see what we shall see!" he grunted and went tearing into the misty oblivion.

From nineteen thousand feet down to an even fourteen thousand, clinging whiteness swirled past his wings. It faded altogether and he went thundering down into a sea of shimmering gold. For a split second or two the eerie, yet glorious, phenomenon made him catch his breath in dumbfounded surprise.

Far to the east, a blazing sun was slanting its glistening rays through a large break in the clouds. And as a result, the under-neath side of the cloud banks were acting as giant reflectors that recast the golden beams earthward.

It was glorious, but also a hell of a nuisance right at the moment. So dazzling was the affect, that the jagged terrain below was practically obliterated by the quivering mantle of golden brilliance.

Instinctively, Dusty pulled out of his dive, cut around sharply and flew straight into the sun. One hand shielding his eyes he held his course for almost ten minutes. Then, waggling his wings in hope that Curly would see him and be on the alert, he swung around, down and back in the opposite direction.

With the sun behind him, the scene below changed consid-erably. He could now see the ground in detail. But as he stared at it a bitter curse rippled off his lips.

Up to now he hadn't formulated any definite ideas as to just what he would see once he reached the Mex-12 area. But now that he had reached his objective he was filled with a sense of utter futility and hopelessness. For there below him, was a horizon to horizon panorama of sun-scorched wilderness. As far as the eye could see in all directions, were foothills, jagged topped mountains and tangle-shrub covered plateaus and valleys.

A look-see patrol over this God-forsaken terrain?

The question brought a harsh laugh to his lips. It would take half a dozen units a month of Sundays to really look this place over. And he had figured that he and Curly would be able to do it without much trouble! Hells bells! He certainly had been mistaken.

But, as Dusty turned in the seat and looked across the air space at Curly's ship flying, which was wing-tip to wing-tip with him, he suddenly caught the flash of wings far to the north. He lost them instantly in the shimmering, golden air, then saw them again—this time clearly.

A flight of ten planes was winging toward him. He started to motion to Curly, but checked himself, for his pal had already seen.

Then, a second later, the signal light on the radio panel blinked and the earphones crackled.

"Calling Captain Ayres! Twenty-fifth Scouts calling Captain Ayres!"

Dusty grabbed for the transmitter tube. The Twenty-fifth was a hard flying Texas outfit, and if that squadron was clawing air his way the patrol might be successful, after all.

"On your wave-length, Twenty-five!" he called. "Go ahead."

He could now clearly see the American ships, with their rattlesnake insignia on each fuselage. And as the ear-phones emitted words again, he knew that they, too, had seen him.

"Joining your patrol, captain. H.Q. orders are to escort you back across the border. We will take up formation position behind you. Then return above clouds."

"What?" Dusty echoed. "Why above clouds? I want to look this place over. Fall in behind and I'll lead."

"O.K., captain," came the cheery assent. "But, of course, you'll have to explain to H.Q. later. Stand by at throttle while we take up positions."

Dusty grunted and automatically cut down the speed of the

Silver Flash. Curly did likewise and together they loafed air as the Twenty-fifth ships swung up to their level and dropped neatly into line position behind them.

"Thank you, Captain Ayres! Now, you will both go down and land!"

The harsh cruel voice in the ear-phones turned Dusty's blood to ice. For nearly three seconds he sat motionless, eyes riveted dead ahead. Then he jerked around in his seat and glanced back.

"Exactly, captain!" grated the phones. "You have blundered into a perfect trap. I knew that you would go through with it, regardless. Now, land!"

AMERICAN SHIPS—TEN of them right back there on his tail. But, there were no Americans riding the cockpits. The snarling voice of the Black Hawk coming to him over the radio smashed home that staggering truth.

"Enough of this delay, Captain Ayres! I order you to land, at once. You are lucky that I spare your life this long!"

The repeated command of the Black Hawk jerked him out of his trance. But he didn't move immediately. However, he did turn his head just a fraction. Enough so that he could see Curly Brooks, off his right wing-tips.

For an instant their eyes met, and each read the thought uppermost in the other's brain. It was a perfect, silent understanding between two sky warriors who had reached the crossroads of life and death.

Reaching out his hand, Dusty eased the throttle back even more and allowed the ship to nose down.

41

"You win this time," he shouted into the transmitter tube. "Down we go—now, Curly!"

He fairly screamed the last. He rammed the throttle home and shoved the stick up against the instrument board in one lightninglike motion. A split second later he thumped down on left rudder and walloped the stick over left. The plane quivered, then pivoted in the half turn of a spin, and as Dusty hauled back on the stick, the nose shot skyward.

Whether Curly had pulled the same "safety" trick he did not know. But there was no time to search air for his pal. The trapping Blacks had careened out of formation and were striving frantically to slam him into oblivion. Through rage-filmed eyes he saw a rattlesnake insignia sweep across his sights.

Vision and action were one. His twin Brownings snarled out a song of certain death. A made-in-America glass cockpit cowling splintered into a million pieces and the head of the murdering Black beneath it was filled with steel.

Dusty didn't wait to see the ship go sliding crazily off on wing and spin down out of control. Instinct told him that he had scored, and he didn't have time to bother about proof.

Many times had he battled the Black Hawk and his flying killers. Sometimes it had been with savage joy in his heart. At other times with nothing but berserk rage gripping him. But this time, all emotion had fled him. He was but a mechanical machine that functioned instinctively.

Even time lost all significance. It was as though the sky battle had started with the very beginning and would continue into eternity. His body was so numbed to any feeling that he barely

DESPERATELY THE BLACK
TRIED TO ROLL OUT....

noticed the fact that twice a white hot coal sliced through his shattered cowling and bit into the fleshy part of his upper left arm.

Suddenly, his blurred eyes focused on something that instantly jerked him back to full consciousness.

That something was Curly Brooks' all blue ship flopping and flat spinning helplessly earthward, with two Blacks pouring streams of steel into it as it went down.

Dusty whipped up and over a Black who was trying to close in on him, and went tearing down in a steep vertical dive. His speed was so terrific that he was pinned against the seat back, and it was all he could do to spin the wave-length dial and wrench the transmitter tube off its cockpit hook.

"Hang on, Curly!" he roared. "Stick it out, kid, I'm coming!"

That Brooks might not be in a position to hear the bellowed encouragement, didn't occur to him. All he realized was that death was reaching out for his pal. The Dayton and Texas-Four disasters were forgotten. So were General Horner and his son, Agent 10. In fact, Dusty's brain could register only the fact that Curly's plane was flopping earthward.

The clatter of his own guns blasted against his ears. Until then he hadn't realized that he was firing. Fighting instinct had made him automatically rudder one of Brooks' attackers into his sights. Triumph surged within him as he saw the rattlesnake plane go skidding and twisting frantically off into the clear. Like steel drawn to a powerful magnet, his next bursts of fire raked the second attacker from prop to tail wheel.

Undoubtedly, the pilot was too intent on making his own

kill to realize that he, himself, was under fire. For instead of streaking out and away, the plane cut in even closer, and Dusty saw the zigzag pattern of holes creep up the turtle back of Curly's fuselage. Howling with rage, he risked one fleeting instant to skid outward, then around in he thundered for a broadside attack.

It was then that the Black saw him. Desperately the pilot tried to roll out and cut back. But he didn't have a chance. Nothing could have withstood the merciless fire that ripped out from Dusty's guns.

Like a relentless buzz-saw, Dusty's shower of steel chewed through dural wings, hammered against armor plating, and found the glass cowling. The nonshatterable glass became criss-crossed with millions of tiny cracks. Up careened the pilotless ship, until it seemed as though it would never stop climbing. Then, as though struck by a giant fist, it half rolled and went roaring earthward to destruction.

"Pull out, Curly! For God's sake pull out!"
THUNDERING THE words into the transmitter tube, Dusty slammed around in a flash turn over his spinning comrade. He was ready to give battle to the other Blacks who were now piling down furiously. Let them come, damn their hides! With Curly in the clear, he was ready for anything.

But a snap glance down, showed his pal to be far from in the clear. Brooks' plane was still spinning helplessly. Down toward the jagged rock hills but a few thousand feet below.

"Pull out—pull out, Curly!" Dusty roared over the air again. "I'll hold them off!"

A few seconds later groaning words came out of the ear-phones.

"Can't—controls jammed! Crash coming! Beat it, Dusty. Beat it, kid, and luck!"

"Luck, hell!" Dusty's shouted words blended in with the rattle of his guns. "Pull that damn thing out, Curly! You've got to do it!"

Something was mumbled back at him in the ear-phones, but he didn't hear it clearly. The savage yammer of aerial machine-gun fire was drowning out all other sound. In double flank formation the remaining Blacks were slamming in on him. His plane quivered and jumped as steel pounded and ripped into it. He dully wondered why he remained in the air.

And then, again, his instinctive fighting ability came to his rescue. Over and around went the Flash on wing-tip. He got a blurred vision of a stream-lined snout spitting flame straight into his face. And in the next instant he was the pivot point of a swarm of twisting and turning sky chariots.

Instead of breaking away he had plunged right into the midst of the attacking Blacks. At such close quarters they were helpless to fire at him for fear of hitting their own kind as well. But he had a skyful of targets.

The realization brought a wild laugh to his lips. And keeping both trigger trips jabbed all the way forward, he went thundering around and around in a tight vertical spiral. Sky and earth blended into one great shadow. At intervals a darker blur whipped before his eyes, to disappear immediately. Twice, a ball of flame slanted outward and down.

Then, finally, when it seemed as though he'd go stark, raving mad if he maintained the maneuver an instant longer, he whipped out and up in a thundering zoom. Brushing his free hand across his eyes, he leaned over to the side and stared down through the shattered cowling glass.

The Blacks were desperately striving to follow up after him. But he gave them only a snap glance. It was what he saw below that jerked the gasp off his lips.

Curly's plane was still flip-flopping downward, and in another moment or two would crash.

True, the tall pilot had managed to haul his bullet-riddled craft out of the flat spin. But that was far from enough. Like a kite that has broken loose from its ground mooring, the blue ship was sliding this way and that; not on even keel for more than a split second at a time.

In an instant, Dusty cast the die for his own immediate fate. They had come to Mex-12 together. Together they would go back, or not at all!

Decision and action merged into one. Oblivious to the fire raking up at him, Dusty slammed the nose of the Flash earthward and went thundering down. Not once did he take his eyes off Curly's plane.

He saw its pilot make one last frantic effort to hold the ship steady for a mush landing. That attempt failed, and the plane kicked over on wing and cut downward like a two-bladed knife. Wings folded back like paper. The tail section snapped off and hung dangling at the ends of taut control cables. Then like a great tired bird, the whole mass went sliding off the sagging trees and onto the ground.

"Curly! Curly, old man! I'm coming!" Saying the same words over and over again, Dusty yanked back the throttle and kicked the Flash around toward a small plateau formation. It was less than sixty yards down the hillside from where Curly had struck. The yammer of machine-gun bullets still sliced down at him from above, but he paid them no heed.

SOMEHOW, HE got down onto the small plateau, and managed to wheel-brake to a full stop. He was less than a dozen yards from the cliff that dropped straight down for well over two hundred feet. Unseen metallic wasps kicked up little eddies of dust as he scrambled out onto the ground. Stumbling to his feet, he raced blindly across the width of the plateau, and charged into the maze of tangled tress and thorny shrubs which covered the hillside.

Brambles clutched at him and tried to hold him back. But with hands running red from scratches he tore his way up the hill. Sharp rocks dug into his shins; right through the leather of his field boots. Roots tripped him up and sent him sprawling countless times. But with indomitable determination, he lurched upward and onward.

Then, finally, he plunged into the clear and practically fell on the pile of wreckage that had once been Curly's plane. Heart cold with fear, he clawed his way under a wing that had crumpled back over the cockpit. It took all the strength left in him to pull the thing clear.

What he saw sent a tremendous wave of relief through him.

Slumped back, and well down in the cockpit, was the white-faced figure of Curly. The man's eyes were closed, but he was breathing easily.

Dusty started hauling Brooks out of the cockpit. But because of the way the plane was lying, half over on its side and twisted under crumpled wings, it was a hard job to drag the lean form clear. Eventually, he succeeded in getting Curly out onto firm ground.

Dusty paused a second to rest. Then he bent over and smacked the flat of his hand against Brooks' cheek.

"Hey! Curly—out of it!"

Blood rushed to the cheek he had slapped. Eyelids opened and dazed eyes glared at him.

"Say? Who the—"

Brooks choked off the rest, and struggled to a sitting position.

"My head!" he groaned. Then suddenly, he looked wildly about, "My God—I crashed!"

"And how!" grunted Dusty. "Get up—see if you can walk."

Slowly Brooks got to his feet, swayed a bit, then steadied himself. The eyes he turned on Dusty were wide with disbelief.

"Hell, I remember!" he gasped. "Controls jammed in the scrap—and I crashed. But you—what the hell are you doing here, Dusty?"

"Think I was going to leave you, stupid?" Dusty snapped at him.

The other half grinned.

"I know, kid!" he got out quickly. "And—oh hell, thanks, But, what next?"

49

"You and I are going to try and make a break for it in the Flash," Dusty answered quietly. "Even with you aboard, the Flash can outfly these—"

He never finished.

At that moment the thundering roar of an airplane engine echoed through the hills. As a cowboy knows the whinny of his pinto, so did Dusty know the sound of his own ship. In a movement that left Brooks flat-footed, he spun around and went stumbling down the hillside. His journey up had been torturous, but he went down through the tangle as though it didn't exist.

As he reached the plateau, his service automatic was cupped in his right hand. Cursing at the top of his voice, he went tearing over toward where the Silver Flash was being taxied around for a down wind take-off. The figure in the cockpit was only a blur to Dusty. Nevertheless, he snapped up his gun and pulled the trigger.

For one instant he saw the white startled face turned his way. Then it was gone from sight as the Silver Flash leaped forward and tore across the uneven surface of the plateau.

Blind with rage, Dusty kept on running, and firing. As he saw the Flash clear its wheels and go zooming high up into the air, something crashed down on the top of his head. Then the earth was no longer beneath him. He was spinning over and over, down into a great bottomless pit.

CHAPTER 5
THE TUNNEL TO HELL

A STRANGE feeling of clammy dampness finally pried Dusty's eyes open. At first he could see nothing. All was bathed in a dull, yellow glow, that seemed to flicker intermittently. He stared at it for a moment, then closed his eyes and tried to remember. Eventually, past details came back to him.

He opened his eyes again. The pale yellow glow still fused everything. But, a moment later he realized that he was looking straight into the reflection of a flickering electric light. He shifted his body, and turned his head away. It was then that he saw his surroundings clearly.

He was in a cavelike room. The floor he was sitting on was made of damp clayish earth. And he was leaning back against one of four walls, all of which were constructed of criss-crossed prop beams set flush against clay backing. The ceiling was built in much the same way.

Directly opposite him was a heavy wooden door. And at the top of the door jamb burned a single electric light.

"Through sleeping? Welcome to—I don't know the hell where!"

The sound of Curly Brooks' voice came to his ears like a clap of thunder. He swung around to his left and saw his pal jack-knifed comfortably in the corner. Brooks was grinning and watching him intently. As Dusty gaped, he spoke again.

"How's the head? You want to thank God, you've got a thick one."

Impulsively, Dusty put a hand to the top of his head. He felt a long gash that throbbed at the touch of his fingers. And when he lowered his hand, the tips of his fingers were smeared with congealed blood.

"When I came to," said Brooks, "I swabbed it as best I could. Thank goodness it isn't deep. But, you sure had me scared for awhile."

"When you came to?" echoed Dusty moving over nearer to his pal. "What the hell happened anyway? All I remember is chasing after the Flash. Then everything went blooey."

"For you and me, both!" granted Brooks. "I legged after you in time to see a Black taking a bead on you with a rifle. As I tried to nail him, the ground came up and socked me. Only it wasn't the ground. A sledge hammer probably—and right smack on top of the old dome.

"When I woke up, we were in here. You were lying on your face and bleeding. God, did that get under my skin! Then I saw it was only a crease, swabbed it, and propped you up. End of the first lesson."

Dusty stared around the queer room in silence.

"No idea where we are, eh?" he murmured.

Curly swore softly.

"Not the faintest! But, it's not Fifth Avenue and Forty-second Street, that's a cinch!"

Getting slowly to his feet, Dusty paused a moment or two, then walked completely around the room, eyes searching the wall. The result was not very gratifying. In the first place; the door was securely locked on the outside. Then he found that movement made the top of his skull feel as though it were being lifted clear of the rest of his head. Gingerly, he eased himself down beside Curly.

"What a sweet help we are to our country!" he grated. Then laughed in spite of himself, "Oh well, we're still alive, and that's something."

Brooks snorted and made little furrow marks in the clay floor with the heel of his boot.

"Yeah," he mumbled. "So what?"

Dusty didn't answer. He sat staring fixedly at the light. Then with a shrug, he turned to his pal.

"It looks like nothing for the moment. So we might just as well kill time checking up on a few things. But, before we start checking, get this, kid. The fact that we're alive means plenty. Whoever nailed us wouldn't have taken the trouble to bring us to wherever the hell we are now, if he didn't intend for us to live a while yet. Get what I mean?"

"Got it," grinned Curly. "And don't worry about me caving in. I'm O.K. But what checking do you want to do?"

"LET'S GO back to just after we left the field," said Dusty. "Don't ask me what, but something dropped in front of me. It looked like a great drop of pale green water. I felt heat, terrific heat. The Flash went cockeyed for a moment, and when I looked for you, you were gone. Couldn't even get you on the radio. What the hell happened?"

Curly Brooks had leaned forward a fierce light burning in his eyes.

"By God, I'd forgotten about that!" he gasped. "I don't know what happened either. One moment I was tagging along behind you, and the next—well, I was spinning down hell for leather and the radio panel was shooting sparks. I'd kept the contact switch open, just in case you wanted to get me in a hurry.

"Well, anyway, I slapped the damn thing off, battled like hell to get out of that spin, and finally made it. By then I'd gone down through the clouds. I climbed back and a couple of crates were scrapping right smack over me."

"Yeah!" nodded Dusty, as the other paused for breath. "Believe it or not, I was mixing it up with the Black Hawk. But, the rat got away from me."

He went on to give a brief report of the strange meeting, and the astonishing announcement that the Hawk had made.

Curly listened with eyes popping.

"But," he asked incredulously, "how the devil could he have known? And that explosion! Hell, I must be going nuts! I'd forgotten that, too. It happened when I was in the clouds. I didn't see anymore than you did. The field at Texas-Four!"

Dusty fumbled for a cigarette, and discovered that he had been stripped of everything, including his automatic. He sucked his lower lip a moment in thoughtful silence.

"I'm not sure," he murmured slowly, eyes agate, "but I think I know how the Hawk found out. And I think that General Horner has taken care of that little item. Did you hear? But of course you did. That relayed order for us to return to base. I think that there's a dead Black agent at Test Field Twelve, right about now."

"Do you mean it?" echoed Curly excitedly. "Who?"

Dusty shrugged.

"Not calling my shots until I'm sure," he evaded the question. Then in a bitter voice, "But what the hell are these Blacks doing? Detroit, Dayton and Texas-Four! What a hell of a mess I've made of things!"

He glanced at his wrist watch and saw that it was smashed to bits. A look at Curly's showed that to be smashed too. Getting to his feet once more, he walked over to the door and studied it carefully. No light showed through the jamb cracks, and there was no keyhole on the inside.

It was stoutly constructed of reinforced oak. But as he inspected the outside rims, the flange beams fitted against the clay earth, a tingle of excitement rippled through him. He turned his head and motioned Curly over.

"A make-shift job for all its apparent sturdiness," he said eagerly. "We must be in some kind of an underground storeroom. Just a temporary prison, or I miss my guess. Look, this clay dirt is like damp putty. I can dig it out with my fingers. You work that side, and I'll work this. Maybe we can scoop away enough to make the door frame fall in."

Curly stared at the proposed job with a doubtful eye.

"And then what?" he grunted.

Dusty turned on him and fixed him with a stern look.

"How do I know?" he snapped. "But I'll be damned if I'm going to sit here and rot, until they come for us!"

Brooks grinned.

"Just getting your dander up," he chuckled. "You work better that way. Let's go!"

In silence they started clawing at the clay soil on either side of the door frame. It was a slow, painful job, and at the end of half an hour they had only made two furrows about four feet long and perhaps three inches deep. Their fingernails were broken and bleeding, and sweat was pouring off their brows like rain drops. Presently Curly swore and stepped back, blood and clay smeared hands hanging dejectedly at his sides.

"Wouldn't make it in a month!" he growled. "God knows how deep this damn wall is!"

Dusty didn't even look at him.

"Get back to work!" he grated. "At least it's something to keep our minds busy, you dope!"

Eyes blazing, Curly tore at his side of the frame, like a dog scooping dirt off a hidden bone. Dusty grinned to himself and renewed his efforts.

AN HOUR passed, or perhaps it was two hours. There was no way of gauging time in that clammy prison. The furrow extended the full length of the door frame, and it was a good five inches deep. And as Dusty continued clawing at the clay soil he suddenly felt that the whole thing was sagging inward.

"We're getting places, kid!" he said excitedly to Curly. "Keep digging, keep digging. We'll make it yet!"

Brooks didn't reply. He was too exhausted to bother wasting words. But just the same, Dusty's encouragement rekindled the spark of energy in him and he virtually flew at his job.

About fifteen minutes later Dusty stiffened with eagerness. One section of the furrow on his side was seven inches deep, and he was able to reach through and hook his fingers around the front side of the frame beam.

"Stand back, kid!" he called softly to Curly. "I'm through, and I think I can pull her in!"

"Me too!" the other breathed back. "Give it all you've got on three. One—two—three!"

On the last count, Dusty braced himself and jerked inward. The massive framework sagged inward a bare two inches. Hunks of clay dropped down from the untouched top flange and showered his head and shoulders.

"Again, kid! One—two—three!"

As they tugged the heavy door made a sucking sound, like a giant pulling his foot out of mud. It jammed and resisted all efforts stubbornly. And then without warning, it fell inward with a dull thud. But as it struck the earth floor there was a sharp pop, a sputter of sparks, and the electric light attached to the top of the frame went out. And everything was plunged into darkness.

"Curly! O.K.?"

"Sure!" came back the hoarse whisper. "Weren't we bright to forget about that light? Now what?"

Crawling over the door, Dusty found Curly's arm and held it in a vicelike grip.

"Hang onto me!" he breathed. "This damn thing's got to lead somewhere!"

"To a nice flock of ham and eggs, I hope!" was the fierce comment from the darkness.

Keeping touch-contact with Curly, Dusty got to his feet and

began to feel his way along what seemed to be a prop-beam braced tunnel leading away from the door. The going was slow because of the darkness. Before he'd traveled twenty yards he'd banged his throbbing head against the low-fitted beams in the ceiling at least a dozen times.

Three times the tunnel turned sharply to the right, and once to the left. It was so black that he couldn't even see his hand in front of his face. Progress went on at a snail's pace, because he kept running his hands along both sides of the dank passage, in hopes of finding another door. But his hopes were to no avail.

Then suddenly, without any warning, the passageway turned abruptly to the right for the fourth time, and far down its length was the faint glimmer of fused light. It was electric light; not the glow of day.

Stopping so quickly that the groping Curly bumped into him and cursed, Dusty peered ahead. A sharp gasp in his ear told him that Curly had seen it, too. A moment later his pal's whispered words checked with the realization that had formed in his own mind.

"That light is reflection from a side room, Dusty! The damn passage goes right past it!"

"Yeah, I know!" Dusty breathed back. "And maybe that'll be our out. Keep close, kid, and get set for anything."

Firm pressure on his arm told Dusty that Brooks was ready. Pausing a second more to gather his strength, he started forward again, stealthily. His eyes were riveted on the opening far ahead, through which poured the fused glimmer.

HE HAD gone less than thirty yards when he heard the faint

rumble of voices. He stopped and listened intently. That the voices came from the room ahead, he was positive. He was also quite certain of something else—the language beings spoken was Spanish.

Though by straining his ears he was able to make out a word here and there, his knowledge of that tongue was so limited that what he did understand made no connected sense.

However, it all made for the definite answer of a question that had been burning in his brain since he regained consciousness—where was he? If those Spanish speaking voices meant anything, he was still in Mexico.

"That's Mex, Dusty!" came Curly's excited whisper. "Can't get much of it, but they're talking about money. They're—by God, hear that? One of them just said something about fifty thousand Gringo dollars for keeping Federal troop patrols out of the Chihuahua hills!"

Dusty said nothing, but his hand gave Curly's arm a warning grip signal to shut up. He was rapidly figuring things out. A few more bits of the weird puzzle had dropped into place. It was only guess work, of course, but he felt positive that he was right.

The Blacks had established a foothold in the desolate hills of Mex-12 area. They had undoubtedly done it with the aid of Mexican bandit gangs—throwbacks from the hordes who followed the outlaw, Pancho Villa, years ago. And the Blacks were paying them off in American money for the job of keeping Mexican Federal troop patrols out of the area.

Clever strategy! While loyal Mexican troops fought scattered

ambushing bands of outlaws, an even greater enemy was for-
tifying itself in the very heart of the country they loved.

With an effort, Dusty curbed his rage. Giving Curly a nod,
he hugged the left wall and moved forward. Closer and closer
he came to the dimly lighted opening, and louder and louder
sounded two distinct voices. And then, finally, he was but two
feet from the edge of the opening. He now saw that it was a
regular doorway between braced clay walls.

Gesturing to Curly to maintain absolute silence, he got down
on his stomach and inched forward. He first got a slanting view
into a large room with boarded walls, ceiling and floor. He saw
a bench and a couple of chairs. Several well filled cartridge
bandoleers hung from a peg on the wall. Then he caught a
glimpse of a black leather boot, and a black breeches-encased
leg.

Hesitating but a split second, he shot his head forward
another inch, took a quick look and ducked back. For a full
minute he crouched holding his breath and straining his ears.
No sound but the continued jabbering of Spanish came from
the room. Letting his breath out in a long silent sigh, he straightened up inch by inch, turned and put his lips close to Curly's
ear.

"Two bandits," he breathed softly. "At a table about ten feet
inside and to the left. Rifles are leaning against the table. Think
they're drinking. When I nod, we rush them. You go to the
right, I'll go to the left. O.K.?"

Brooks formed a silent "O.K." with his lips. Dusty grinned,
gave his arm a reassuring squeeze, then slowly backed to the

opposite side of the passageway. He looked at Curly for an instant, braced both hands and a foot against the wall—and nodded.

The two bandits heard the scuff of feet, and spun around in their chairs. By then it was too late. Like an avalanche, Dusty slammed down on his man and carried him sprawling over backward onto the floor. Hissing curses blasted in his ears, and sledge hammer blows rained down on the back of his neck and shoulders.

For one awful moment he believed that he had tackled a job far greater than his sapped strength could manage. The squirming figure under him was a raging tiger, clawing and slashing at everything within reach of his hands.

Through a red film, Dusty saw the glitter of a knife blade. Like a flash he twisted to one side, jerked up his right leg and kicked out. His foot crunched against bone. There was a howl of pain, and a thin blade went slithering across the floor. Dusty threw himself over flat, brought up both his fists and slammed them down upon a distorted white face.

Again and again, he pounded and hammered down on that face. Then, presently, he realized that the figure under him had gone limp and lifeless. Choking, panting for breath he started to his knees, but froze motionless as the harsh words cracked out behind him.

"Enough of that! Hands up—both of you!"

CHAPTER 6
BLOOD EAGLE

TO DUSTY, the harshness of that voice was the same as the whole room caving in on him. For several moments his brain refused to register a thought. It was as stunned and paralyzed as his body.

"Hands up, dogs! At once!"

Hardly realizing that his body was in motion, Dusty straightened up, raised both hands above his head, and deliberately turned around. The steady muzzle of three rifles were trained dead upon him and Curly. Behind the rifles, half crouched three cruel-eyed, Black infantrymen. And behind them, a man with a face twice as cruel—the Black Hawk.

For perhaps half a minute, the ace pilot of the Black Invaders feasted his blazing eyes upon the Yanks, then he stepped around the three soldiers before him, clicked his heels and gave them a mocking salute.

"Greetings, fools!" he jeered. "Greetings and sincere salutations! A pity you wasted so much useless energy."

He smiled, switched his eyes to the two Mexican bandits stretched out on the floor, and deliberately spat upon them.

"Sleeping swine!" he snarled. "You would wag your split tongues!"

With that, he whipped out his automatic, took careful aim and buried a bullet between the eyes of each Mexican.

"You dirty rotten killer!"

Curly Brooks' voice rang out. Dusty saw him leap for the

Hawk, and he yelled a warning. But the warning was too late. Like a cobra, the Hawk darted to one side. The soldier nearest him, swung his rifle. There was a sickening crunch as the heavy barrel hit Brooks and sent him spinning into a corner. In that same second Dusty was in motion. But that motion stopped abruptly. In fact, two gun muzzles digging into the pit of his stomach, stopped him cold in his tracks. Helpless to do anything, Dusty stood there trembling with rage, bloodshot eyes boring into the Hawk's sneering face.

"Rat!" he choked out. "It'll come back to you double, so help me!"

The Hawk's sneer broadened. He walked over, motioned Dusty's guards back, and trained his own automatic on the Yank's tunic front.

"So you have said before, Captain Ayres," he purred easily. "And, good fortune has given you the opportunity to try. But, luck will not last forever, my friend. And by that, I mean this is our last meeting."

Icy calmness settled over Dusty. He relaxed, deliberately jammed his hands in his breeches pockets, and grinned.

"That's nice to know, anyway," he replied. "Decided to let Mex bandits take over for you, eh? Can't swing things alone any longer?"

The other matched his easy smile.

"So you heard what they talked about? Well, it's partly true. For the time being, it serves our purpose to pay these swine to see that we are not molested. But when the time comes, we

"HANDS UP --- BOTH OF YOU!"
DUSTY FROZE MOTIONLESS.

shall swallow up the whole country, just as simply as we have swallowed many others."

Dusty took his eyes from the man's face and glanced at the two murdered Mexicans.

"And that pay is not in dollars but in bullets, huh?" he murmured. "Well, I must say that's your style."

"They were to prove their worth, and didn't," the Hawk answered calmly. "They preferred to wag their tongues, instead of stopping your escape. Why do you think I put you in such a place where escape would be so easy? To test their vigilance! Well, they failed. And to us, death is the price of failure."

Dusty hardly heard him. He was staring anxiously at Curly in the corner. The lean pilot had regained consciousness. He was sitting, rubbing the side of his face, and glaring up at the armed guard who stood over him. For an instant Dusty caught his eye, and in that instant he flashed a "take it easy" warning to his pal.

"—and if money means more to them than strict obedience, then that is their misfortune," continued the Hawk.

"Yeah, sure," mumbled Dusty, trying to recall what the other was talking about. Then, a thought came to him.

"Your boy friend at Test Field Twelve got caught," Dusty said.

To his dumbfounded surprise, the Black Hawk nodded.

"So I heard. But he is only one of many. In fact, Test Field Twelve is no more."

Dusty stiffened.

"What? What the hell do you mean?" shouted Dusty.

The other gestured with his free hand, palm downward.

"Your Dayton Field, your Texas-Four Field, and Test Field Twelve are no more," he said evenly. "They have been removed from the face of the map, as many others shall be removed. And with your Air Force virtually nonexistent, the task we started some months ago will be completed in very short order. Without sufficient planes, your armies will be helpless," the Hawk smiled tightly.

Dusty stared at him and thought of Test Field Twelve, of Major Trapp, of General Horner, and all the others he had left there. Then, suddenly, he gasped and blurted out the question before he could check himself.

"But what about Detroit?" he began. "There—"

A fierce light leaped into the Hawk's eyes as he choked off the rest.

"Ah!" The word was little more than a whistled exclamation. "What about Detroit, captain? That interests me very much!"

Dusty kept his face expressionless, but his heart was looping over. So—the Hawk was curious about what happened at Detroit, eh? Perhaps he didn't know what actually did happen.

"Why ask me?" he countered craftily. "I thought you always claimed to know everything."

The Black bent his ugly face closer.

"Eventually we do, captain," he got out in a gritting voice. "But for the present I'm demanding your story of what happened at Detroit. I know what should have happened. But, it did not. And a man, closest to me of all others, did not come back. Now, tell me!"

Dusty's spine tingled with wild excitement. His pot-shooting in the dark was bringing results. Though the idea was indeed ridiculous, he could not beat back the feeling that he was getting closer to the answer of the greatest mystery that had ever confronted him. Why? Because the Black Hawk was puzzled. Puzzled and worried over something. And when the Hawk was that way, he talked more than he meant to.

For several seconds Dusty looked him straight in the eye. Then he hunched his shoulders and grimaced.

"O.K., if you must know," Dusty said. "We caught your pal and gave him a little rough-on-rats. Well, he talked—to save his rotten neck. Told us about your plans—this new idea of yours. Why do you suppose I came way down here—to paint pictures? Stupid, you're on the wrong end of the limb, and you know it!"

Like a statue of stone, the Hawk stood staring at him. Not a muscle of his face moved. It was as though he had been suddenly struck dead, and was kept standing by invisible props. Then slowly dull crimson seeped up his neck, over his jaw, and on up his cheeks to the roots of his scraggly jet black hair. Before Dusty could even think about dodging, the Hawk whipped up and slashed his gun against the Yank's temple.

"A lie, you dog! That is a lie!"

The words came to Dusty only as a faint distant rumble of sound. Like a log he went crashing down on his side. Instinctively, he threw out both hands and checked his fall somewhat. For several minutes he lay sprawled out, trying desperately to fight back the giddiness that swirled about him. Eventually, he struggled grimly to his feet and stood there swaying and glaring defiantly at the hawk-faced figure garbed in black. His tongue felt as though it filled his entire mouth, and he practically hissed out the words.

"Have your fun, while you still can! It won't be long, now. You're sunk, and your number's going up fast!"

The Hawk's derisive laugh floated across the room to mock him. A laugh that was both scornful and gloating, but with also, just a faint tinge of relief in it. Then the Hawk walked over again, close.

"Do you know why it is a lie?" he snarled. "Because the man we speak of was a deaf mute. And you, dog, tell me that he told of my plans. But, you ask, why do I suppose you came down here?

"I'll answer that. It was because another fool like you succeeded in sending through just enough information to cause your cursed superiors to be interested in this particular part of the world. But that dog did not sent through the important information he possessed. We were able to prevent that. You came down here because of the message Agent Ten sent to General Horner. Or should I say, what Agent Fifteen sent to General Horner?"

Dusty stared at him dull-eyed as the truth seeped into his brain. The Hawk saw the look on his face and sneered gloatingly.

"I am right, yes?" he asked. Then answered his own question, "But I always am! And from that moment, our eyes were on General Horner, on General Bradley, on Major Trapp, and on you. A shame that the X-Rayoscope was destroyed, eh? It will take you some time to construct another one. And then it will be too late. You should have made more than one in the first place!"

Dusty started inwardly at the last remark. So, the Hawk didn't know about the first X-Rayoscope plane? Was there possibly any connection with X-Rayoscope plane Number One and the Hawk's wonder about what happened at Detroit?

The idea that had been drifting about in his brain for a long time, suddenly became stationary and took on faint tangible form and meaning. He sucked in his breath sharply, then exhaled it in a chuckle as he suddenly realized that the Hawk's eyes still were boring into his own.

"Wrong again, dummy," Dusty lied. "I admit that we got one message that was garbled. But, you see, Agent Ten sent through complete details a bit later."

The Hawk's reply to that was to shake his head sadly from side to side. In fact, it was exactly like an unhappy parent shaking his head at the actions of a wayward child.

"You continue to lie, captain," he said. "And I assure you, it makes no impression upon me at all."

Dusty forced himself to continue the bluff, if for no other reason than to gain time. Out the corner of his eye he could see Curly Brooks slowly bracing his body against the two walls that formed the corner. And the lean pilot's eyes were fixed steadily on the pit of the stomach of the Black who guarded him. Recognizing the symptoms, Dusty knew instantly that Curly was going to let fly any second now. He groaned inwardly at the man's foolhardy intentions, but nevertheless steeled himself to be ready to do his part.

"That's what you think," he grinned at the Hawk. "How many times has Agent 10 tripped you guys up? Too damn many to count!"

And then the Black called his bluff.

"History is unimportant," he said. "It is the present that concerns us most. But you may wish for proof of what I have said. And so you shall have it."

Keeping his gun and eyes on Dusty, the Black shot a queer jabber of strange words out the corner of his mouth. Instantly one of the guards came forward, and pinned the Yank's arms behind his back, and lashed them securely.

"Just in case your desire to be foolish, continues," the Hawk smiled at him. "Now march through that door. And don't forget that there is a rifle no less than six inches from your back."

Dusty hesitated, looked at a door on the opposite side of the room, to the left of where he and Curly had entered, and then he glanced sidewise at his pal. For an instant as their eyes met, Dusty shot him another warning. Then blinked stupidly as he heard the Hawk's chuckle.

"Don't worry about your friend, captain. He'll be well looked after. And we won't be long. Now, march forward!"

With a shrug, Dusty walked through the open door and started down a long dimly lighted passageway that seemed to extend endlessly. It was constructed much the same as the room he had just left; heavily boarded all around. As he shuffled along, he mulled over a thousand and one new thoughts that crowded into his head. They were not pleasant. Particularly the thought of Agent 10. In the back of his brain had been lingering the tiny hope that fate had not really overtaken his comrade of former adventures. But now, that hope had died. The Black Hawk's own words had killed it. No doubt about it—they had caught Agent 10. Perhaps played him as a cat plays a mouse, and then destroyed him.

"Stop, captain. We go in here!"

The Hawk's command pulled Dusty up short. They had reached a door leading off to the right. It was an ordinary wooden door, reinforced with strips of iron. Yet, as Dusty stared at it dully, a sensation of reluctance rippled through him. Perhaps it was more of a feeling of dread. What was beyond that door? So strong was the feeling, that he unconsciously stepped back until the muzzle of the guard's gun, in the small of his back, checked him.

At that moment, the Hawk stepped around him, selected a key from a bunch he pulled from his pocket and inserted it in the lock. The click of the lock tumbler falling free was like the shot of a gun in Dusty's ears. He instinctively stiffened and squared his jaw.

Hand on the knob, the Hawk paused and smiled at him triumphantly.

"And now, captain," he purred, "the absolute proof that you seem to need."

With that the Black flung open the door. At the same instant the guard gave Dusty a shove that sent him stumbling into a brilliantly lighted room.

Dazzling light was his first impression. The next was temperature. Dusty felt as if he had stepped from a stuffy attic into a cold storage plant.

And then, the third and final impression. Rather, it was a stark reality that froze him solid to the spot, and seemed to squeeze his pounding heart to a bloodless pulp. Against the far wall of the room, sat a man in civilian clothes. The man was staring glassily at him. And that man was Agent 10.

For a moment the room reeled around in topsy-turvy circles. It was all Dusty could do to remain on his feet. He felt that he was looking at a ghost. Agent 10 sat rigid in his chair. His hands were folded in his lap, and one leg was crossed over the other. Were it not for his eyes, the man might be asleep.

"Jack—Jack!"

Dusty's choking moan echoed about the room. The Hawk laughed harshly and gave him a little push.

"Perhaps your friend did not hear you, captain!" he sneered. "Get closer to him!"

Dusty stumbled and almost pitched forward on his face. As it was, he went to his knees less than a foot in front of the motionless man in the chair.

"Jack—Jack, old man, what have they done to you? What have they—?"

He finished the rest in a rasping gasp. His face went white as he stared at his friend. He shook his head and closed his eyes.

"No, no!" he groaned. "My God, no!"

He opened his eyes again, and the horrible truth mocked

A RIFLE BARREL GLITTERED IN THE LIGHT AS IT SLICED DOWN.

him to the very depths of his soul. The man in the chair was stone dead, and his lifeless body embalmed.

With the cry of a wounded animal, Dusty lurched to his feet, spun around, and wrenched savagely at his bound wrists.

"You cursed dog!" he flung at the smirking Hawk. "You—you rotten, filthy swine! I'll kill you! So help me God, I'll kill you!"

Swept off his feet with blind rage, he rushed at his hated enemy. The Hawk laughed horribly and smashed a fist into his unprotected face. And as Dusty reeled, the Black hit him again. Arms pinned securely, he was helpless to save himself, and went crashing down onto the floor.

Features distorted with gloating hate, the Hawk stood over him, reached out a clawlike hand and curled his fingers into a fist.

"Like that his feeble life was squeezed out!" he grated. "And so shall it be with you. Too long have you both annoyed me. But now—now the final triumph is mine. Think back, you dog—back to the time I first captured you. I told you then that you were going to our museum of war prisoners.

"You were to go there alive. It is different, now. You shall go there a dead man. You shall go with this other fool. Preserved for all eternity, and for all to look upon. And pictures of you two shall be dropped upon every square foot of your cursed country, so that your comrades may see and realize what is in store for all those who fight against me!"

The man fairly screamed the last. Half turning, he pointed a trembling finger at the dead man.

"Look at him, now!" he snarled. "The great Agent Ten, son

of the great General Horner. For the last time he has tricked me. Never more shall we wonder about him. His thread of life has been cut. Look at him! Eyes that see nothing. Lips that cannot speak. Arms that cannot move. And legs that cannot walk. Look at him, and see yourself as others shall soon see you!"

The Black finished with a wild waving gesture of his arms. His eyes blazed red like sunken pools of fire. His lips curled back taut over fanglike teeth. And his whole body rocked and swayed and trembled with uncontrollable triumph.

Crumpled on the floor, Dusty watched his actions with pain and sorrow-dulled eyes. Every thought had fled his brain leaving it stunned and blank. Though his very life depended on it, he could not have moved a single muscle at that moment. He simply lay there watching—watching a blood-thirsting madman weave and sway about.

And then like a flash, it happened.

Something behind the Hawk moved—like a streak of lightning. A rifle barrel glittered in the light as it came slicing downward. Then there was a sharp smack as it hit the Hawk behind the right ear. The Hawk stiffened. His eyes widened and lighted up with dull surprise. Then he half turned on one heel, and went crashing down on the floor.

"Well, kid, that evens up the clout they gave Brooks!"

CHAPTER 7
THE SECRET OF EL JATATE

THE WORDS rang like fire-gongs in Dusty's head. Through gaping eyes, he stared at the cruel-featured Black guard, who now stood grinning down at him. He started to speak, but no words came. His mouth had gone bone-dry, and his tongue was stuck to its roof. He blinked stupidly, tore his eyes from the grinning guard, looked at the dead man in the chair, then back at the guard again.

"You—you—you—"

He could go no further. The room started spinning. From a thousand miles away he heard a voice.

"Hell, yes! Here, hold steady while I cut these damn ropes. There! Easy, now—just sit up!"

Dusty's brain was still spinning furiously. Rubbing his numbed wrists, he sat staring stupidly from the guard to the dead man in the chair, and back again.

"It's—it's your voice, Jack," he mumbled thickly. "But—but, I don't get it. Don't get it at all!"

"Don't try for a minute," came the answer. "Here, take a swig."

Dusty gulped down liquid fire from a flask the other put to his lips. A warm comforting tingle rippled through him. His head cleared, and he could feel strength coming back. Slowly he got to his feet, and stood with his back against the side wall. The dead man in the chair was still a powerful magnet. He pointed his finger.

"Then—then who's your double, Jack?" he got out with an effort.

The one dressed as a Black guard didn't answer for the moment. Instead, he took the ropes that had bound Dusty's wrists and pinned the Hawk's arms behind his back. With the man's own belt, he jack-knifed the legs and bound the ankles to the wrists. Then he stood up, and looked at Dusty.

"My double?" he echoed. "One of the finest lads that ever breathed!" he went on fiercely. "He died a brave man, and by God, if I killed every rotten Black rat alive, I still wouldn't be able to even up for him."

The man suddenly stopped short, and squared his shoulders.

"But there's still plenty to do," he said grimly. "Pete wouldn't want me to blubber around like this. First, tell me everything from the start, Dusty."

Dusty shot a glance at the door, looked at Agent 10. The Intelligence man shook his head.

"I locked it," he said bluntly. "And it's sound proof. Go ahead, give me everything from where you started."

Speaking in clear, crisp sentences, Dusty related everything in detail from the moment he received General Bradley's order, right up to the present moment.

"Now, it's your turn, Jack," he finished up quickly. "For the love of God, what's it all about?"

The other hesitated and grimaced, bewildered.

"Frankly, I don't know," he began.

"But that message you sent through!" cut in Dusty. "It said—"

"I know what it said," the other interrupted right back. "Now, hold your shirt on, while I begin at the beginning. Pete—"

Agent 10 paused long enough to look at the dead man in the chair.

"Pete and I," he went on savagely, "were working on another job back of the Black lines up north, when we happened to get wind of something being planned down here in Mex-twelve. How we got it doesn't matter. In fact it was little more than a hunch. However, we followed it up and discovered that the Blacks were making nightly transport flights to some place. And those transports weren't filled with troops, either. They were loaded with equipment, machinery and parts.

"Transports would leave one night and return empty the next. At that time, of course, we didn't know exactly where they went. In other words, we had no definite information to send through to Washington H.Q., so, we had to play the thing alone."

YOUNG HORNER paused, and stared at the floor as though trying to recall details.

"There was only one thing to do," he continued suddenly. "That was to make a trip aboard one of the ships. Besides the pilot they carried a crew of two men. Well, one night about ten days ago we succeeded. A couple of rats were removed, and Pete and I took their places. The pilot made a flare landing at a spot about five miles south of where we are right now."

"By the way, where are we, exactly?" put in Dusty.

"In the middle of nowhere," the other snapped. "Shut up until I finish!"

Dusty grinned and gestured compliance.

"And then we stubbed our toes," Agent 10 went on ruefully. "Instead of waiting and playing it safe, we tried to beat it as soon as the plane landed. The pilot got suspicious, and—well, we had to plug him and run for it. God, run for it in this damn forsaken place! Anyway, we were able to get clear and hide. But, the cat was out of the bag, then.

"The Blacks knew that someone was getting their smoke. From then on we were walking on dynamite. To stay holed up, in between a couple of low hills, meant getting nowhere and eventually starving to death. So—well, there was nothing to do but risk mingling with the Blacks."

"Yes?" echoed Dusty eagerly, as the other paused again. "What did you find out?"

"Nothing, and everything," was the startling grunted reply. "We found out that something was going on in a hill west of here called El Jatate, I believe. Black labor troops and some Mexican bandits were continually swarming all over it, carting the stuff up from the drome and taking it inside the hill. Just what it was all about, we never found out. That is, exactly. To come within two miles of the place meant death.

"Guards had been placed all around the hill, and luckily we found out that every man working in that hill was known to them. Here's an idea of just what I mean. I saw a group of drunken Mexicans—some of the very band that's keeping Federal troops out of the hills—stagger over that way, and get mowed down without even a challenge."

"My God!" breathed Dusty. "But wait a second. If you came

down in one of the ships, you must have seen the stuff that it carried. Couldn't you get any idea from that?"

"That's what I'm leading up to," nodded Agent 10. "The stuff we saw, besides the machinery and parts, was drums of rocket gas and drums of Tetalyne."

"Tetalyne?" cried Dusty. "Are they planning to blow up Mexico? Why—"

He suddenly cut himself off, and stared hard at Agent 10.

"Good God!" he breathed hoarsely. "I wondered—had a hunch—but hell, I thought I was crazy. Do you suppose—is it bomb rockets?"

Agent 10 shrugged.

"God knows what it is!" he said harshly. "But they've got something—something that blew up the air bases at Detroit, Dayton, Test Field Twelve and Texas-Four."

"But hell!" burst out Dusty, as though the other had put up an argument. "They couldn't have done that with bomb rockets! A bomb rocket wouldn't even reach Texas-Four, from here. And my God, Detroit is a good two thousand miles away. Incidentally, they didn't hit Detroit, as I told you. There was a terrific explosion, but it was up above the clouds. But, go on. Didn't you find out anything else?"

"Nothing, except that they planned to wipe out all Central States air bases. And that the destruction of the Detroit base was scheduled for seven last Monday night."

Dusty stiffened.

"Last night, you mean, don't you?"

"No, Monday night," said Agent 10, shaking his head. "You

were out for a day and a night—both of you. But to get on with it. By piecing together a word here and there, we realized that an attack was to be made on the Central States air bases. How or what, we didn't know. But we did know that something was up, and that Washington should be warned.

"Pete and I drew straws to see who would make a dash for the border and get word through, using my new number, and who would stick here."

The Intelligence man paused and turned sad eyes toward his double. When he spoke again, there was a catch in his voice.

"Two days later Pete came back—dead. His disguise had been stripped off, and he was dressed as you see him now. God Almighty, I almost went mad. I was in the very room when one of their agents told the Hawk how they had caught him, and had managed to garble the teletype message enough so that all of it didn't get through. And I was there later when word came through that you and Brooks were coming down here. Had I had half a chance, I would have killed the Hawk right then and there. But, I didn't.

"I just had to stand there and take it. Stand there and curse myself to hell and back for ever letting Pete talk me into the double idea. You see, we'd known each other for years. Entered the service together. A million times we've been taken for twin brothers. God—"

The agent blotted out the rest with a choking sound. Dusty stared at him a moment, then took hold of his arm and pressed hard.

"Chin up, guy!" he said harshly, and hating himself for it. "Like he'd want—no blubbering. There's a job to be done!"

The other nodded silently. A strained look on his face, for all of its make-up.

"The first thing, is to get Curly," Dusty went on speaking rapidly. "But listen, I'm asking you again, where are we? In some kind of a clay house, or what?"

"We're in a hill they've tunneled out for living quarters," said Agent 10. "Remember that place in Canada, where we were just before the Duluth show? Well, this is like that, only they haven't bothered to build it up like they did that underground radio power station. That's what worries me. I'm damn sure that this is only a temporary idea. And, unless we work fast, well—"

He shrugged and left the rest hanging in mid-air. Dusty nodded.

"Just one more question, before we go to work. Those ships from the Texas Twenty-fifth—how—?"

"They're not Twenty-fifth ships," Agent 10 cut him off. "That's how Pete and I got our first hunch. We saw those ships assembled on the Hawk's drome in Canada. Saw them even paint that rattlesnake insignia on each one."

Dusty frowned.

"Hell, I don't get that!" he muttered.

"I do," said the other. "I heard them joking about it. They use the bandits to keep the Mexican regular troops out of the hills. And they use these ships to wave away any of our pilots who might happen to wander down this far. Just a blind, I figure— Huh? What's the matter?"

83

Dusty had grabbed him by the arm, and was pointing with the other hand.

"The door!" he breathed. "We're having company. See? Someone's trying the knob!"

It was true. The inside knob was slowly turning. Then it stopped, and there sounded a faint creak of wood. Like someone putting his shoulder against the other side.

"Get back, out of line!" grunted Dusty.

WITHOUT WAITING to see if his friend obeyed, he bent over, scooped up the Hawk's gun, and went stealthily over to the door. Silently he eased off the lock. Then tightening his grip on the gun, he jerked open the door with his other hand, and stepped back. A grunt, and a figure came spilling inside. Dusty's upraised gun was halfway down before he checked himself.

The squirming figure on the floor, striving desperately to leap up, was Curly Brooks.

"What the hell?" gasped Dusty, and slammed the door shut.

Brooks gaped at him, let his eyes flash about the room, and returned them to Dusty's face.

"What the hell, is right!" he snorted, getting to his feet. "A damn wonder I didn't plug you as I came in. I—God, who's that?"

He pointed a finger at the dead man in the chair. Dusty told him in one crisp sentence.

"He was Jack's double!" Then added, "And this is Jack."

"Huh? Huh?" Brooks gulped in amazement. "My God, am I going nuts? You're—you're—"

"Right, Curly," nodded Agent 10. "But how in God's name did you get here? What about those two guards?"

The lean pilot glared at Dusty, and addressed his answer to him.

"Think I was going to let that tramp walk you out on me?" he snapped. "Hell, some one had to look out for you. So, I faked a faint, clipped one of those mugs, and put my foot in the other's face. When the bell rang, papa had both the guns. That fact, and a little physical persuasion, induced them to tell me where I'd find you. And—well, it looks like you didn't do so bad, yourself."

"But the guards, Brooks?" cut in Agent 10 nervously. "Where are they now? Did they escape?"

"Escape?" snorted Brooks. "Don't worry, those two Mex eggs are wide awake, compared to them. But, listen, what's the dope here? So what?"

Cutting it down to the bone facts, Dusty told him the story. Brooks' eyes went agate, and he drew a bead on the unconscious Hawk.

"I'm going to love this!" he grated. "You guys have been wasting time!"

Like a streak of light Dusty shot out his hand and knocked the gun down.

"Cut it, you damn fool!" he barked.

"By God, yes!" chimed in Agent 10. "When he comes to, and realizes, I'm the one that'll pull the trigger."

"And the hell you will!" Dusty whirled on him. "My God, are you saps both crazy? Jack, give me that flask!"

Agent 10 just stood there glaring at him in frowning puzzlement. With a quick motion Dusty snatched the flask from his hand, knelt down beside the Hawk and forced some of the liquid between his fang teeth. Then setting the flask on the floor, he deliberately released the man's arms and legs.

Agent 10 cursed, and grabbed his arm.

"Ayres!" he grated. "What—My God, I tell you I'm going to kill him! I'm going to let him know and then kill the dirty, rotten skunk!"

Dusty shook off the hand, stood up and fixed the Intelligence man with a steady eye.

"Listen, kid," he cracked out, "we've all been through hell, and it's no time to go haywire now!"

"But Dusty!" the other protested wildly, "what in God's name are you doing?"

"Using my head!" the pilot snapped. "Now, cut the questions! You and Curly get back to that other room and lug those two stiff Mexicans here. Get going, dammit!"

More words were on Agent 10's tongue, but Curly grabbed hold of him and pulled him toward the door.

"Come on, Jack," he said. "That guy's stubborn as a mule, but he's usually right. Let's go!"

The three or four minutes that they were away, Dusty spent in feeding liquor drops to the Hawk. And by the time they returned, lugging the Mexicans by the shirt collar, the Black was groaning softly, and moving his head from side to side. "You watch the Hawk, Jack!" ordered Dusty tossing him the automatic. "But don't shoot, or I'll break your neck. You, Curly—strip! You and I are going to borrow these Mex outfits."

"Listen, Ayres, damn your soul!" flared up Agent 10, as Dusty and Curly stripped and climbed into the dirty regalia they took off the dead Mexicans. "What in hell is this all leading up to?"

"The answer we want is at this hill, El Jatate, isn't it?" the ace shot at him.

"Yes, I'm damn sure of it!" grated Agent 10. "But what has—"

"Plenty!" Dusty cut him off, buckling a cartridge belt and shifting it so that the holstered gun swung easy on his right thigh. "We're going to take a look at El Jatate, and find out things!"

"But you crazy idiot!" the Intelligence man shouted back at him, "didn't I tell you that only selected ones can get near the hill?"

"Sure, you did," Dusty nodded calmly. "But I'll bet my shirt—my own one—that the Hawk, here, knows all the passwords and all the high signs."

Agent 10's eyes flew open wide, and his head bobbed forward. "Huh?" he choked out. "You mean—?"

"Right!" Dusty shut him up. "We're going to make a personally conducted tour of El Jatate, and this rat is going to do the conducting!"

CHAPTER 8
SATAN'S TRAP

IT TOOK Agent 10 a minute to let the truth sink all the way in. Then he gasped, and smashed his clenched fist against his leg.

"My God, am I dumb!" he exclaimed. "Hell—maybe there is a chance!"

"Maybe?" snorted Dusty, as he unholstered his gun. "Maybe hasn't got anything to do with it, kid. It's fact! Now, you two keep your traps closed, and let me do the talking."

Squatting down beside the Hawk, he slapped the man's face twice, sharply. The Black groaned louder, half raised a protesting hand.

"Out of it!" Dusty barked at him. "We're going places, and we're in a hurry!"

The words must have penetrated the Black's dulled senses, for he opened his eyes, stared glassily at Dusty. Then suddenly, the glassy look faded away, rage took its place, and the Hawk started to squirm. As he did, Dusty deliberately gun-whipped him across the bridge of his nose. The Hawk yowled with pain and fell back.

"That's better," Dusty grated. "I feel mean today. Maybe you know why? Here, have a drink. You're going to need a clear brain to get what I have to say!"

The Hawk cursed violently, but tilted the flask nevertheless. "Dog!" he hissed, hurling the flask from him, "watching you die will be doubly sweet after this!"

Eyes hard, Dusty gun-whipped him again.

"Shut up! I'm doing the talking. Sit up, and button back your big ears."

Backing off a pace or two, Dusty waiting for the Hawk to sit up. The man's eyes blazed with rage, and seemed to almost spit fire as he saw Agent 10. A string of words, Dusty couldn't understand rushed off his lips. But he got a good idea, as Agent 10 answered in English.

"No, you skunk, you won't do a thing. I'm not one of your rotten kind. Guess, damn your soul—guess who I am?"

The Hawk went rigid. Puzzled eyes whipped over to the dead man in the chair, whipped back to Agent 10's face. Puzzled eyes they were, but in their depths Dusty saw a glow of phantom fear. He laughed harshly.

"The great Black Hawk who sees all and knows all!" he grunted derisively. "Didn't I say you were on the wrong end of the limb? Tough, isn't it?"

The Black's face was purple with rage. The veins at his temples stood out like cords and his doubled fists went white at the knuckles. He looked just like what he was—a trapped cobra whose venom has been drawn.

"Just keep your eyes on this, tramp!" clipped Dusty, patting his gun. "One dizzy move, and it goes boom-boom. Now get this—we'd like to have a look at El Jatate, see? Ah! Sure, of course, we know all about it. More than one can play your game you know.

"But, as I was saying, we're making up a little party to inspect this El Jatate hill. And as we might have trouble going over to it, why you're going to act as our host and guide!"

The Black's lips curled back in a scornful snarl. The cobwebs of unconsciousness had cleared away from his brain, and a look of cunning was creeping back into his eyes.

"Fools!" he spat out. "I will have you all shot!"

Smack!

Dusty's gun bounced off the man's nose for the third time. Blood spurted and dripped down his tunic front. He started to scream curses, but the motion of Dusty's gun hand stopped him instantly.

"I hadn't finished," said the Yank coldly. "You're going to be

our host and guide, and you're going to make damn sure that the hired help doesn't try to get rough. Because, if they do. If they even bat an eyelash the wrong way, this little gun I have here, is going to plant a slug right between your beautiful eyes!"

"You'll die!" the Black hissed venomously. "My men will kill you on sight!"

Dusty shrugged and cocked an eyebrow.

"That's the chance I take," he said, "Maybe they will kill me. But get this—two of us will die. And the other will be you! Now, take that as a bluff, or kiss the book on it for a fact, it

makes no difference to me. But, if I get it, or any of us get it, there'll still be a slug for that spot between your eyes."

AS HE finished the Yank straightened up. Still keeping his eyes on the Hawk, he half turned his head and shot words out the corner of his mouth at Agent 10.

"Jack! You know the way out of here, don't you?"

"Yes. The passageway leads straight—"

"O.K., then," Dusty cut him off. "Take Curly's gun and walk on this rat's left. I'll walk on the right. Curly—you lug the rifle and be rear guard. And Jack—you know the Black lingo. If this lug says the wrong thing to anyone we meet, let him have it. Got me?"

"You're damn right, I have!" grated Agent 10, cold, narrowed eyes riveted on the Hawk.

"O.K.!" Dusty snapped at the Black. "On your feet. You know your part in the act. Better make it good!"

The Hawk got slowly to his feet. There was a faint smile on his cruel lips. To Dusty that smile was like a red flag of warning. He walked close to the man, and tapped the gun barrel against his chest.

"Last warning!" he said in calm, deadly tones. "One dizzy trick, and you get something I've been saving up for a long time!"

The other sneered.

"You will never leave this place alive!" the Hawk snarled. "None of you will live to see another day!"

Dusty made no answer. He was through talking. He had warned the Hawk, and he knew that the Black believed him.

Perhaps it was insane, this plan he was going to carry out. But, he could think of none better.

Past experience had proved to him that at heart the Hawk was yellow. Though he killed ruthlessly, he safe-guarded his own life with almost fanatical fervor. Chance and sacrifice had no part in the man's code of self conduct. Yeah, as long as the Hawk lived, the three of them would live. Yet—

He shrugged aside the tiny and persistent doubt that trickled through his thoughts, and nodded toward Agent 10.

"Let's go," he grunted. "Curly, hold the door open."

His gun alert, Dusty motioned the Hawk to move forward. The Black hesitated, then smiled and started walking. Planked on either side by a grim-faced Yank, he went through the door, turned right and started down the long passageway. And then began a journey through the very realm of Hell, itself. Each yard seemed a mile long, and each second an eternity of nerve wracking strain.

Trusting to Agent 10 to make sure that the Hawk took the right course, Dusty concentrated on watching the man. Out the corner of his eyes he caught snap visions of doors, intersecting passageways, and braced ventilating air shafts down through which filtered the faint light of day outside.

On impulse, he holstered his gun, and a few moments later he was glad he had, for the passageway suddenly opened up into a big subterranean room. In it two Black soldiers were seated before a large radio panel. Phones were clamped over their heads, and they were both bending over transmitter tubes.

To the right of each man was a wireless key, clamped down for the moment.

But, as the inspection party entered the room, the Black radio operators looked up, recognized the Hawk and leaped stiffly to attention. Dusty's heart pounded furiously, and he gripped hard on the butt of his holstered gun. Eyes glued to the Hawk, he mumbled incoherent Spanish words, and acted as though he were totally unaware of the presence of the radiomen. But his skin twitched and tingled with expectation. If those radiomen got suspicious—if they—

But, they didn't. Without even jerking his eyes toward them once, the Hawk walked across the room and through the door on the opposite side. As Dusty heard Curly close it, he breathed a long silent sigh of relief.

"That was swell!" he murmured in the Hawk's ear. "Just be sure that you keep up the good work."

A soft, purring laugh came from the Black's lips. It served to increase the doubt that still stuck in Dusty's head. In fact it took complete possession of him for the moment. One danger spot had been passed. But it was nothing compared to what lay before them—two long miles of Black infested ground, and a solid ring, so young Horner had said, of guarding soldiers who shot to kill on the slightest suspicion.

Hell, he was mad—mad to be leading Curly and Jack to a very probable death. The idea had been all his. He'd simply barked orders at his two pals, and they were obeying him blindly. Putting their trust in his snap judgment. Trust? Hell, they were staking their lives on that trust.

DUSTY GRABBED the Hawk with his free hand and jerked him to a stop. He saw Horner's eyes jerk toward him. For an instant he met that look.

"Maybe I'd better do this alone," he grunted. "You two make a break for it, once we get out in the open. Get through to the border. Better yet, maybe you and Curly can grab a two seater from their drome. You know where it is. Use my official number and order every damn bomber within range to come down here and blow this place off the map. I'll try and join you later."

Agent 10's eyes were watching the Hawk, but his words came at Dusty.

"Don't be a fool!" he snapped. "You'd never make it alone. And we wouldn't quit now, even if we were sure of it. We stay! Come on, around that bend is the main entrance at the base of the hill."

Torn between the truth of Agent 10's words and reluctance to permit them to possibly toss their lives away for no other reason than a blind sense of loyalty to him, Dusty started to speak again.

"Save it, kid!" Agent 10 stopped him.

With a shrug Dusty nudged the Hawk onward. And two minutes later they rounded the bend in the passageway and came upon a wide cross-beamed opening. It opened out onto a small sun-baked valley. Beyond were rugged, scrub-covered hills, some higher than others, save for that fact each was practically a parched and barren replica of the next. As Dusty stared at the scene, he dully wondered how in the name of God,

Agent 10's double had been able to find his way back to the Texas border.

And then he stopped wondering, tensed himself as a Black soldier stepped into view from around the corner of the entrance, and came stiffly to attention. But, once again, the Hawk didn't

THE SILVER FLASH

even look at the man and passed him by as though he didn't even exist.

A moment later, Dusty suddenly realized that the Hawk had drawn away from him, and was bearing to the left and toward the upper end of the valley. He closed up the gap in a flash, and glanced questioningly at Agent 10.

"We headed right?" he grunted.

"Yeah," the other nodded. "El Jatate is that third hill over there—the highest one. The guard ring is just back of this first hill."

Dusty took a look in the direction his pal pointed. As far as he could see, El Jatate was just another hill. True, a tall one, tall enough to be classed as a mountain, but nothing more. Like all the others that rolled away to the four horizons, El Jatate had been untouched by Nature's paint brush, and left to the mercy of a relentless sun.

To think that that jagged hunk of ground contained the solution of a hellish mystery, was almost beyond belief to Dusty. Though he strained his eyes at it, he could see nothing to quicken his pulse beat. Nothing moved on it. Not even the withered and snarled shrub growth, for there was not even the memory of a wind about.

And then, suddenly, he forgot all about El Jatate and stopped dead in his tracks. From out of the blazing sky had come the throbbing beat of an airplane engine. Louder and louder it grew. And the sound was like drum beats in Dusty's head. Sound only, but he knew beyond all possible doubt that the Silver Flash was in the sky.

A moment later, confirmation that Dusty did not need, presented itself. From over the hills to his left, came glistening silver wings. The nose dipped down, then up and over the plane slid in a graceful half loop. It rolled off the top, and spun around in a whipping dime turn. And from that it fluttered into a falling-leaf.

"The Flash! Damn his soul, what's he doing in my crate?"

Dusty blurted out his thought savagely. Then the Hawk's purring chuckle made him look at the man.

"What's he doing, you ask, captain?" smirked the Black. "He's simply enjoying himself. You see, the plane has served the purpose of its capture, and so I have given my pilots permission to fly it. You know, the Silver Flash is not exactly unknown among us."

"Served its purpose?" Dusty glared at him. "What purpose? Out with it, before I—"

"Steady, Dusty!" came Agent 10's hissing warning. "That entrance guard is watching us!"

"Exactly!" the Hawk sneered into Dusty's face. "It would be unpleasant should you forget yourself, now. You would be caught in your own trap. Its turn and turn about, captain. While I live, you live. And while you live, I live."

DUSTY IGNORED the hidden meaning in the words. He was furious at the thought of the Flash being in the hands of others.

"I'm still asking you," he grated, as they moved onward. "What purpose?"

The Hawk smiled to himself, and shrugged.

"That, captain," he said softly, "is something you will find out, possibly, at a later date."

For one moment Dusty had the desire to gun-whip the truth from the man's lips. But, fortunately, reason curbed the mad desire. There was more than just himself to be considered. Curly and Agent 10 were there, too. And so, crushing the urge, he walked forward, gun ready and eyes fastened on the Hawk.

As they reached the upper end of the valley, they came upon a narrow dirt road that seemed to wind in and out, endlessly, among the hills. Six different times they met groups of Black soldiers and Mexicans, wandering along with rifles unslung.

Each time Dusty's nerves tightened to the snapping point, and he felt that he was walking along the crater of a volcano. Yet, nothing happened. No one spoke to the Hawk. They simply stiffened to attention and saluted as he passed by, and ignored them completely.

And though the incidents made Dusty's heart thump with increasing hope, the feeling of doubt grew proportionately stronger. For one thing, it was all going along too nicely. Too damn nicely! From the way the man had acted at the start, he knew damn well that the Hawk didn't want them to see any part of El Jatate at close range. Yet, his attitude had suddenly changed once they started. Passing within two feet of his own soldiers, he had not so much as given them a single glance.

In fact, the Hawk had quickened his pace, as though anxious to get past them and onward. Was it because the Hawk feared the results, should his own kind speak to him? Feared that bullet marked for the spot right between his eyes? Or was there some other thought in the man's brain?

Over and over again Dusty asked himself those questions and failed to answer any one of them. He searched for a possible answer in the expression on the Hawk's face, and in the look in his deep sunken jet-black orbs. But there, also, he failed to get an answer. And then he dismissed it from his mind and concentrated on the job ahead.

They had rounded the base of the second hill and were approaching El Jatate. Nearness brought out only one fact that Dusty had not noticed before, because it was hidden by the other hills. And that was a large opening cut into the base of the hill.

It was about twice the size of the opening in the other hill, and the ground in front of it was covered with tread marks from puppet tractors. There were a few box crates lying about, and just inside the opening Dusty could see drums of liquid Tetalyne, the most powerful explosive known to man.

Yet, strangely enough, there was not a single guard at the entrance. Save for the drums of Tetalyne and the glow of electric light bulbs inside the entrance, it could well be the adit of an abandoned mine. And it was the absence of any guards that sent a strange tingle rippling up and down Dusty's spine, and caused him to come to a halt, and check the Hawk.

"Just in case your hearing is bad," he grunted at the Black, "I'll repeat my warning. Any tricks, and you get it first, so help me God! Jack—Curly, on your toes, now. If we meet trouble, split up, and make for the Border, as I said. I'll handle this egg. Get it?"

"Got it," they murmured together.

Then Agent 10 added, "Let's go!"

"That's your signal, bum," Dusty nodded at the Hawk. "Move—and remember—"

For obvious reasons he left the rest hanging in mid-air. But the Hawk only smirked and walked into the tunnel. As daylight was left behind, the feeling of doubt in Dusty swelled up more than ever. A sense of warning shot through him, and seemed to touch every nerve in his body. He silently cursed himself for losing his grip, and clamped down hard on his jangled nerves. No matter what the cost, damned if he was going to turn back now.

Before him lay the end of the trail. He was sure of it. A thousand different deaths might be awaiting him, and Curly and Jack Horner. But that was the risk they were taking. Rather, the risk he had suggested, and they had instantly agreed to take.

Dayton, Test Field Twelve, and Texas-Four! Was the answer to those three mysteries to be discovered before he saw the light of day again? As he moved along the wide passage, he turned that question over and over in his mind.

Then without warning complete dizziness engulfed him. There was a great roaring in his head, and he could no longer see. His brain was flashing orders to his trigger finger, but that finger was unable to move. In fact his whole body was paralyzed.

He tried to cry out, but no words came. He seemed to be hanging in mid-air—floating halfway between the floor and the ceiling. His vision cleared for an instant and he knew that he was looking up at a light bulb in the ceiling. Then everything fused into pitch darkness, and he dropped down—down—down.

CHAPTER 9
PARA-GAS

THROUGH A blurred fog, Dusty heard a voice cursing bitterly. The tone was muffled and indistinct, but cursing, nevertheless. Shaking his head, the pilot dug knuckles into his eyes. The fog that swirled before them vanished.

He found himself staring at Agent 10. Young Horner's Black Invader make-up had been removed and there was a nasty gash just in front of the right ear. The Intelligence man was half slumped against a wall, pounding his fists against each other and cursing violently.

Dusty stared at him in amazement for a second, then reached over and grabbed the man's arm.

"Hey! Button it up, Jack!" he snapped. "What the hell's the matter?"

Agent 10 jerked his head around, fixed him with dazed, bloodshot eyes.

"Matter?" he echoed thickly. "My fault—all my fault! I saw it—realized too late."

"Huh? You—"

Dusty cut himself off as memory piled back. He gasped, his eyes roamed around the room. It was something like the room in which the two Mexicans had been shot. He glanced down at his clothes and saw that he still wore the Mexican outfit. And. Agent 10 was still clad in Black Invader uniform, even though the make-up had been removed from his face.

Then truth hit Dusty like a bolt of lightning. Curly Brooks was not in the room!

"Brooks!" he choked out. "Where's Brooks?"

Agent 10's eyes widened in dumbfounded realization.

"By God, that's right!" he gasped. "Brooks isn't here. Oh my God! If only it had been me instead of Pete!"

The man started trembling. The dazed look in his eyes deepened and he began opening and closing his fists. Dusty saw, and recognized instantly, that Agent 10 was fast approaching the limit of human endurance. He was on the verge of complete collapse. Drastic action was necessary.

Like a flash, Dusty shot out his hand and smashed the palm against Agent 10's face. Young Horner fell over on his side like a ton of brick, and lay there, staring up at Dusty. Then his eyes lost some of their dazed look, and a bit of color seeped back into his chalky cheeks. Slowly he sat up.

"Thanks a hell of a lot, Dusty!" he got out in a low voice. "I needed that plenty. Hell, must be losing my grip, or something!"

"Not a chance!" Dusty snapped him up. "But, what do mean about this all your fault stuff?"

"That gas band," the other said. "I saw it—"

"That what?" Dusty interrupted.

"Gas band," Agent 10 repeated. "There was a band of gas stretched across that tunnel. Para-gas they call it. It paralyzes the nerve centers almost instantly. I ran into it once up in Canada. Didn't you see the vent on each side of the tunnel?"

Dusty shook his head.

"Guess I was too busy watching the Hawk," he grunted.

"Well, there were vents," replied Agent 10. "One on either side running from the floor to the ceiling. The gas makes a circular course—out of one vent, across the passageway, and then up and over, through blower pipes above the ceiling, and down out through the vent again. It's an invisible door through which no one can pass unless they know it's there."

"And of course the Hawk did!" groaned Dusty. "Hell, now I understand why he toed the mark for us so nicely. He lead us into a perfect trap!"

"Just that!" echoed the other savagely. "But the hell of it is that I should have noticed the vents. If I'd only realized just what they were in time, I could have stopped it."

"But the Hawk?" asked Dusty. "He was shoulder to shoulder with us! Why—"

"Para-gas is harmless unless it gets into the lung tissues," explained Agent 10. "He probably just held his breath until we went cold. It would only have been a matter of thirty seconds at the most."

DUSTY'S HEART suddenly leaped with faint hope. "Curly!" he exclaimed. "Curly was a couple of paces behind us! Maybe he didn't get it. Maybe he plugged the Hawk, and—"

Agent 10 shaking his head, stopped him.

"Now you're slipping, kid. Take a look around!"

Dusty scowled at him.

"I don't get you!"

"Then figure it this way," replied young Horner. "How'd we get here? That door over there is locked. I tried it a few minutes ago."

As Dusty looked toward the door, his hopes died. Was there but one answer? Had the Hawk grabbed a gun and shot Curly? And now the Yank's dead body lay somewhere outside there, under a blazing sun—with vultures circling greedily down toward it?

He groaned, and cudgeled his temples with his fists. Dammit, he was doing just what he'd reprimanded Horner for—letting himself go. But he mustn't. Hundreds, maybe thousands of men had died by now—and that terrible toll would be increased. He knew that. And he also knew that it had to be stopped.

Stopped? The word tantalized and mocked his determination. Stopped? Why, certainly—but how?

He cursed softly, lowered his clenched fists and looked at young Horner.

"How long have you been conscious?" he asked.

"About a minute or two before you came around," was the answer.

Dusty sighed.

"Then you don't know where we are, or who brought us here?" he grunted. "Your make-up's been removed, you know."

"I know that," the other nodded. "But it's the only thing I do know. Except, that my head feels four times its normal size. Must have struck something as I went down. Or maybe I was clouted one."

Agent 10 let his voice trail off. Dusty started to speak, then checked himself. What was there to say? They both knew the same things, and no more. They were prisoners again. But Curly—what had happened to Curly?

Then, suddenly, there came the muffled sound of a shot beyond the door. A split second later there was a faint gurgling noise and the door shook as something struck it.

As one man, Dusty and young Horner leaped to their feet, and stood rigid, eyes flashing the same question at each other. From beyond the door came a scuffing sound, then the jingle of metal pieces hitting against each other.

Unconsciously, Dusty moved back from the door, and waved Agent 10 back, too. Then on impulse he sidled over to the man, bent his head close.

"Down, Jack!" he whispered. "Down on the floor, as if you were still out. When I yell, go for the nearest one. It's the only chance we have. Somehow I don't think they're going to fool around with us any more. Give 'em hell, anyway—and luck!"

Agent 10 didn't answer. He simply gripped Dusty's hand hard, and then sank down on the floor. Dusty did likewise, and flung one arm over his head to half hide his eyes. Then holding his breath, he waited tensely. A key was grating in the door lock. It was turning. The tumbler fell free with a sharp click and the door was opening!

What happened in the next second astonished Dusty so that he gasped. It jerked him up to a stiff sitting position, and set his heart pounding furiously.

Brooks—Curly Brooks was entering the room and lugging

106

a limp Black infantryman after him! Blood dripped from the lean pilot's left hand, and the gaudy Mexican blouse sleeve was stained a dull crimson. Curly's face was chalky and strained, but his eyes were bright and brittle. He let the dead Black sag down onto the floor, flashed a grin at Dusty, and then whipped a silencing finger to his lips.

"Save it!" he whispered. "You two O.K.?"

WITHOUT WAITING for their nods, he tossed a gun to each of them, and beckoned. The feel of a gun in his hands gave Dusty a new feeling of confidence. Trust Curly to come through in a pinch! He leaped to his feet and followed Brooks' motioned instructions to go outside. Agent 10 was right at his heels.

Curly brought up the rear, closed the door, twisted the key in the lock and jerked it out. Then scooping up a rifle that was leaning against the side wall, the lean pilot swept them both with a warning look.

"Shut up, and follow papa!"

In Indian file, Curly first, Dusty next, and young Horner last, they started down a dimly lighted, winding passageway. It was fiendishly hot, and Dusty sensed that they must be dose to the surface of the ground. But a moment later dank cool air struck his cheeks. Brooks had turned sharp right and was leading them down a long flight of steps cut into solid clay. At the bottom he turned sharp left, and then right again into a pitch black tunnel.

As Curly's groping hand came back and touched him, Dusty grabbed it, stuck his gun in his shirt front, and put his other hand in back of him. Agent 10's found it, grabbed hold, and in chain fashion, the three of them moved forward through the darkness.

Presently, Dusty's straining eyes saw faint light filtering into the passageway far ahead. He must have stiffened, because Curly's hand gave his own a warning squeeze. Or, perhaps it was a reassuring squeeze. He didn't know which. But with heart thumping and eyes glued ahead, he moved forward.

The light seemed a thousand miles away. Dusty had the wild impulse to make a dash for it. But he curbed the desire and forced himself to match his pace with Curly's. Then, finally, they reached the light. Curly stopped and turned toward them. His face looked whiter than ever, but his lips were curled back in a satisfied grin.

"End of the line," he whispered. "We all get off, here!"

For a moment, Dusty made no comment. His eyes were sweeping about the room in which he found himself. About a quarter of the way down the right wall from the ceiling, a boarded box shaft extended upward at a twenty degree angle. It was down this shaft that the light filtered. And as Dusty stooped and looked up the shaft he saw dull sky, tinged with a few faint streaks of crimson. Night was closing down fast.

But as he switched his eyes back, he noted that on the far side, two tunnels, similar to the one through which they had entered, led off into a black unknown, at forty-five degree angles. Then he suddenly realized where they were.

They were in the distribution center of an underground ventilating system. Air came down through the shaft that slanted upwards, and then was passed along through each of the three tunnels leading outward. But—

"How's this for apples, kid? There's our out, or I miss my guess!"

Curly's whispered exclamation jerked Dusty out of his reverie. He took hold of his pal's arm, then let go quickly as his fingers touched wet blood.

"You're hurt!" he breathed fiercely. "Here, hold still. Let me have a look!"

The other pulled away.

"Forget it!" he hissed. "Just a crease that bled a lot. But it's O.K., now. Your boy friend's a rotten shot."

"But—what—how?" began Dusty, excitedly.

"Luck," the other grinned. "Dumb luck. I saw you lads stagger. He grabbed you, nailed your gun, and we fired together. Then hell popped. A million guys came piling down the tunnel. I ducked back, started to run for it, bumped into some kind of a door and fell through it. Black as the inside of your hat.

"I picked myself up and peeked back. They were lugging you and Jack down the passageway. And a couple of more of them were carrying the Hawk. He was out—or dead. Guess that's why they didn't start looking around for me. Didn't know I was about."

Curly paused, licked his lips, and widened his grin.
"SO I ups and goes along with them," he continued. "There were two or three Mex lads along, see? So what the hell, who'd notice one more? Anyway, we went through doors, up stairs, and all over God knows where.

"Then the lads carrying the Hawk went down one passage, and the lads lugging you boys went down another. I followed you. They were doing something to you, Jack. Pulling at your face, or—"

Curly stopped and bent close to young Horner.

"Oh, I get it! They tugged off the make-up. Anyway, they all finally reached that room. I hung back then. Had a hunch they were going to park you awhile.

"Remember those stairs we came down? Well, I practically fell down them. The change of air got me thinking. So, figuring I couldn't get near you lads for a while, anyway, I did a little exploring and found this place. Then I went back. They'd parked a guard outside the door. I tried to jump him—and muffed. I had to shoot. Took his keys, and here we are."

"But these guns?" whispered Agent 10 as the other paused. "Where—?"

"Yours went flying as you dropped," the lean pilot cut him off. "They left it where it was, and I scooped it up. Had my rifle anyway. And the guard I plugged had the gun you've got now. But, what happened to you guys? You went out like a couple of lights!"

Dusty told him in a few words. Then young Horner added to it.

"They must have shut the gas off when they came up. That's why you didn't catch it when you followed them. Or maybe the Hawk turned the valve as he went down. Only a whiff was needed, anyway."

"God, kid!" husked Dusty, gripping Curly's good shoulder. "Thanks! Neither of us will ever be able to even up for this!"

"I should say not!" chimed in Agent 10. "Not in a hundred thousand years!"

Brooks glared at them both.

"Cut the sob stuff!" he grated. "Aren't we all in the same pot? Nuts, think I was going to run home to mother? You two have saved my hide enough times. But, forget it.

"Look, I figured this out, too. That shaft is about the length of two of us. We'll boost one man up into it, then a second guy can hang onto his feet, and the third lad can shove him. In that way, the first guy will be able to reach the lip and pull himself out. Then he can pull up the second and third guys. Simple as hell. And we can do it, too!"

Dusty nodded slowly. He had been thinking about that very possibility. But as he stared at the shaft now, there was another thought in his mind. It had come about as the result of realizing that they were still in hill El Jatate. Now that they were inside, why toss away that advantage by going outside? There was still the mystery of El Jatate to be solved.

"Well, don't I get a medal for that?" came Curly's irate whisper. "It's a cinchy way out. Soon it'll be dark, and there'll be nothing to it!"

Dusty grinned and gave him a playful poke in the ribs.

"You rate more than medals for what you've done, kid!" he grunted. "And your idea is swell—perfect. But—"

"But what?" demanded Curly.

Dusty didn't answer for a moment He stood scowling at the

111

air shaft. Then he motioned the other two into a huddle in the corner.

"Listen to me, fellows," he said softly. "All of us playing the same idea is risking too much. Granted that you, Curly, pulled a miracle, it's possible that we all might get nipped next time. And speaking of time, we've used up a lot and haven't got very far.

"Now, we're all of us damn sure that the answer to something mighty big is here in this El Jatate hill. So, it's time for us to split up, and work different angles."

"Like hell!" broke in Agent 10. "We're—"

"Shut up, Jack! I mean it! I'm positive! Now, here's the plan. You two will go up that shaft when it's dark. Jack, lead the way to the drome. As I suggested before—grab a ship and let Curly fly you to the border. Once there, you can contact your dad and get a raid started down here. At the same time your dad can arrange to have the Mexican Federal forces started up from the south. Hell, they can't stay out of the war now.

"Anyway, the point is, to blast this place off the map. Maybe, this damn mystery will go up with it. But, that doesn't matter, as long as this place is wiped out. My guess is that there are not enough Blacks around here to give our bombers and troop transports much trouble."

"Check on that last," nodded Agent 10. "But, grabbing two planes is just as easy as grabbing one. I think you ought to come with us. We'll all make a break together."

"YOU'RE MISSING the point!" whispered Dusty fiercely. "I'm not saying that you will get a ship. It's just another line of attack for us. It—"

"But you can't stay here, Dusty!" Curly took up the argument. "I don't know whether I killed the Hawk or not. But, the rest of them are going to find out that you've escaped, and they'll go through this place with a fine-toothed comb. And then where—"

"That's what I'm counting on," Dusty silenced him. "I hope they do find out that Jack and I have escaped. That will concentrate attention here, and give you two a better chance of reaching the field and getting a plane. Don't you see, we'll be playing two different angles toward the same objective: wrecking this place.

"Maybe I'll get a break and be able to do something here. This is where I headed for in the first place, when we knew even less than we do now. But, at the same time, you two will be trying to make contact with the outside, and get help started down here."

"I think it's my job to stay," spoke up Agent 10 doggedly. "You two are both pilots—that'll make it easier getting a plane. One of you at least should get through. And besides, I've got a personal score to settle with that rat—if he's still alive."

Dusty took hold of his arm.

"Personal scores, be damned!" he snapped. "I'm thinking of Dayton and Test Field Twelve, and Texas-Four—and what may happen. You've got to go, Jack. You know the lingo, if you and Curly meet anyone. And you know how to get through to your dad, once you reach the border.

"Good God, Jack, you're the key man of the three of us. If anyone can get through, it's you. And it's Curly who'll do the flying if that's the way you break. If not, then at least there'll be two of you against any odds. A chance to split again, and hope that one will still get word through. Get it?"

Agent 10 scowled at the floor, and said nothing. But Brooks nodded slowly.

"I do," he said. "And Dusty's right, Jack. I don't want to leave the big ape any more than you do. But, he's right. We're getting nowhere, all of us working the same angle."

Young Horner heaved a long sigh, and shrugged.

"Yeah, maybe that's true. Guess I'm thinking too much about poor old Pete. God, if I ever do catch up with that rat again, I won't even wait to let him know!"

"And my slug will be right beside yours, kid," echoed Dusty. "But the way you can best serve Pete's memory is to go through with my suggestion."

He paused and suddenly realized that very little light was coming down through the shaft. So little in fact, that the faces of his two pals were just shadows in the deepening gloom. He leaned forward and tapped them both on the shoulder.

"Time to go, lads," he said quietly. "A million in luck. And when it's all over, the drinks will be on me."

Silently they all stood up. The air had suddenly become charged with excitement. Dusty could feel his own body shiver, and he cursed silently.

"I'll go first," sounded Horner's whispering voice. "Better

save that arm all you can. I'll take your rifle. And, you—see you soon, kid."

The last was for Dusty. He felt the other's groping hand, clasped it hard, and said nothing. A queer lump in his throat blocked, made silence imperative. He simply nodded, made a step with his hands, and gave Agent 10 a boost up into the shaft. The man wiggled up a way, and waited for Curly to grab his feet.

"O.K., Curly," Dusty whispered, as the lean pilot hesitated.

"Right!" came the acknowledgement. "But, listen, bum, it's only because I'm damn fool enough to believe in you. However, I'll be back—and soon! I must keep an eye on the boy. He's liable to get the one-man army urge too often, you know!"

Dusty chuckled.

"Up with you, tough guy!" he grunted. "Or I'll take back my promise and stick you for the drinks!"

Brooks snorted and reached up for Agent 10's boots. Then with Dusty as a foot brace, he shoved himself up into the shaft, and in turn helped young Horner to wiggle his way up to the top.

"O.K.!"

The word drifted down to Dusty, to let him know that young Horner was out. An instant later Curly's boot soles drew away from his pushing hands. A moment or two more of soft scuffing sound, and then silence. Curly was out.

Fists doubled, teeth clenched hard, Dusty deliberately turned his back on the shaft opening and stood staring at the dark blotches in the gloom that were the three ventilating tunnel outlets.

CHAPTER 10
THE DEVIL'S WORKSHOP

F OR ALMOST five minutes, he stood motionless, battling grimly with his thoughts. With Curly and Agent 10 beside him, his plan had seemed perfectly sound. But, now that they were gone—well, it was as if the bottom had dropped out of everything. Had he unwittingly sent his two friends to their death?

Such thoughts whipped through his brain. Then, suddenly, he was on the alert. Harsh cries came drifting to him from out of the darkness.

At first he thought that they came from outside, and his blood went cold for fear. Curly and young Horner had been caught. But a moment later he realized that the noise came from up the tunnel; the one he had traversed a short time ago. That could only mean but one thing—their escape had been discovered, and the search was on.

Thought and action crystallized into one. Gun in his hand, he went down on all fours, made a quick choice of the two free ventilating tunnels and ducked into the one that lead down and to the right.

It was pitch dark, and he couldn't see a thing, but the shouting behind him egged him on at a reckless pace. The tunnel twisted and turned endlessly. Half a dozen times cool air swept the back of his neck, and without bothering to explore, he guessed that he was passing air shafts like the one Curly and Horner had climbed through.

As he crawled onward, he sensed that he was going deeper and deeper down into the hill. What lay ahead, he had no idea. He only knew that as yet he had not come upon any lead-of-passage; only feeding shafts that slanted upward. That fact made him believe that he was in the main tunnel of the entire system.

He had long ago lost the shouting voices. But, that didn't cause him to slacken his pace. If they had discovered the escape, they would leave no stone unturned. Therefore he was working against time. Working for what?

The question echoed and re-echoed in his mind as he scrambled onward. He didn't try to answer it. He was making a blind stab at the solution, and there was no telling what the next five seconds might bring to pass. His only comfort, if it could be so called, was the knowledge that he was inside hill El Jatate.

Suddenly, he checked his pace and crouched motionless. To his ears came a faint whirring sound, like some dynamo running at terrific speed. And to his nose came the rancid smell of waste oil.

There was another odor mingled with it. A bit gassy it seemed, but he couldn't tell for sure. As he slowly straightened up, the smell grew stronger. It seemed to come from his left.

Shoving the gun in his shirt front for the moment, he turned and groped about with both hands. Rough hewn prop braces met his touch. Then he felt an opening in the wall. It was about two and a half feet square. Just barely large enough to hold an average sized man—and a rather tight squeeze for him.

Sticking his head and shoulders inside, he wiggled all the way in. The smell was stronger than ever. It made his nose itch and his eyes smart. But, like a bloodhound who has picked up the scent, so had he caught the scent of a definite objective!

He knew beyond all possible doubt that the smell was from some kind of machinery—the machinery Agent 10 had seen transported from the drome to the hill. That alone, was enough to force him to risk his chances in the narrow tunnel.

Presently the smell became so strong that it gagged him, and he had to ram a dirty Mexican handkerchief into his mouth to muffle his coughing. His eyes burned, and his whole body became ringing wet with sweat. But he crawled and wiggled onward.

Then the tunnel veered sharply to the right and down. So abrupt was the change of course, that he slid forward a good three or four feet before he was able to stop himself.

HE FOUND himself gaping down into a large, and brilliantly lighted room, that contained all manner of machinery. Among other things he saw a lathe, a drill press, a steel stamping machine, several dynamos of varying size, a riveting hammer, and a wall bench covered with countless types of tools.

He swept them all with a glance, and fixed his eye on an oil and grease smeared Black mechanic who was bending over curved sections of bright green material in the corner. What the stuff was, he didn't know. They might have been sections of steel or laminated wood. At any rate they were all painted a brilliant green, and every edge was flanged and grooved. And the Black, a whirring electric screwdriver in his hands, was screwing locking lugs in place along the flanged edges.

Trembling with excitement, Dusty stared at the green sections and wracked his brain for their meaning. Each was a different shape and length. How they would fit together, and what they could make, was beyond him.

Then the Black had laid down his electric screwdriver, and was walking across the room—walking toward a point directly below where Dusty crouched! The man had only to raise his eyes and he would see the Yank braced in the narrow, slanting vent shaft.

And that was exactly what the Black did. Jet eyes flew upward, and met his. For a second they filmed with dumbfounded surprise, then—

Dusty didn't wait for the next move. He dug sidewise with both feet, braced them against the wall and shoved with all his might. At the same time he shot out both hands in front of him.

Like a torpedo leaving its firing tube, he came out of the vent shaft and down onto the Black. Through blurred eyes he saw the man tug at his jumper pocket as he stumbled over backward. The next instant something glittered in the light. Then he saw no more as they crashed down on the floor in a heap, and he ducked his head.

Something sharp slid across the back of his neck, and he felt the collar of his shirt rip free. Flinging out one fist he smashed it down against yielding flesh. His other arm was pinned under

119

the Black. Hoarse, rasping sound filled his ears. He smashed his fist down again, and then hurled himself to the right. Momentum pulled his pinned arm free, and he went bouncing up on his feet.

GENERAL HORNER

FIRE-EYES

He got the flash glance of a snarling face, and a big hairy hand gripping a long, steel trench knife. It curved his way. He stumbled back, dodged to one side, and slammed into the work bench. He stumbled back over it, and as his head snapped back, he saw steel slice past him and dig deep into the wall.

Twisting to the right, he threw himself down onto the floor, and jerked his gun from out of his shirt. A huge mass rushed at him. He swung down and sidewise with his gun barrel. There was a sharp thump, a gasping groan, and the gun went flying out of his fingers. He tried to duck to the side, but stumbled and then went flat as a falling body crashed down on top of him.

For a moment he lay panting and choking. His head whirled and it felt as though a thousand devils were pounding it. He felt as though he would never be able to get on his feet again. And for a few seconds he didn't care. He wanted to close his eyes and go drifting off on a great soft cloud of blissful unconsciousness.

"Up—up, you fathead!"

His own voice sounded in his ears. Barely realizing what he was doing, he pushed the limp form of the Black off his chest, and struggled painfully onto his feet. Drunkenly, he lurched across the room and picked up his gun where it lay in a corner. Then turning, he went back to the Black. The man was mumbling to himself, and moving his head from side to side.

As Dusty reached him, his eyes fluttered open. The Yank knelt down beside him.

"Sorry!" he grated. "But you're too tough to fool with any more."

With that, Dusty brought the gun barrel down on the mechanic's head. A cool, deliberate blow that landed just above the right ear. The Black's eyes snapped shut, and a long sigh whistled off his lips. He went limp once more.

Dusty stared at him, and nodded grimly.

"Sweet dreams!" he muttered. "And maybe I'll be around when you wake up!"

Grabbing the mechanic by a hand, he dragged him across the room and slung him behind the long, thick base of a drill press. Then steadying himself a moment, he turned and walked over toward the green sections the mechanic had been working on.

CLOSE INSPECTION brought out two things. One, that the sections were made of corrugated dural, and braced on the inside by curved I beam steel girders. Secondly, that each piece was numbered at both ends. That fact served to confirm the belief that the pieces could be fitted together to form some sort of a solid oval framework.

For a long time he stared at them, and pondered. Finally, he shrugged, shot a quick glance around the machine shop, and let his eyes come to rest on a door. He started toward it, then froze in his tracks. There were voices beyond the door—and they were getting louder and louder.

For one split second he hesitated, then leaped across the room and virtually threw himself behind the steel stamping machine. Hardly had he drawn his feet up under him, and hidden himself behind the wide base, than the door creaked and swung open. He could just see about three inches of the bottom of it.

As it swung wide, the Black Invader jabber came clearly to his ears. Not knowing the language he paid it little or no attention. His eyes were fastened on the bottom of the door. It swung shut and he saw two pairs of black leather boots. One pair, though, was about twice the size of the other. Then as a harsh voice boomed out, his heart seemed to stand still.

Fire-Eyes, supreme commander of the Black Invaders, was in the room!

The truth crashed through his head like the roar of a thousand cannons. He could only see part of the man's boots, but he didn't need to see more. Only one man in all the world had a voice like that. And that man was Fire-Eyes, the man of mystery and self-styled destroyer of modern civilization.

Fire-Eyes down here at Mex-12—down here in hill El Jatate.

His heart was pounding so furiously, it seemed ready to burst. Memory of everything that had happened was blotted out of his brain, by the one all-engulfing realization that mankind's most cursed enemy was there in the room—and that he, Dusty, had a gun.

He tightened his grip on the butt, and curled his forefinger about the trigger. Madness? Perhaps, but his hatred of the Black Hawk and the rest of his brood excluded all other consideration. Kill Fire-Eyes and wipe from the world the most terrible destroyer since the beginning of time!

Breath clamped in his lungs, and gun-hand rock steady, he slowly leaned over to the right. He saw the big boots, and the coarse black bloomer breeches. He also saw the other pair of legs, but only as far up as the knees. An overhanging shelf of the stamping machine cut off further view.

To shoot he would have to expose himself entirely. A tremor ran through him at the thought. Fair enough! He'd get the two of them. Oh God, make the bullets go straight. The fate of one hundred and forty million people was depending upon this one moment.

Hesitating a second, he steeled himself, and then—

He went rigid. The door had slammed open, hiding Fire-Eyes'

legs. A voice rasped out harshly. There was the booming reply from Fire-Eyes. At the same instant feet pounded against the floor. And as Dusty hurled himself out from behind the stamping machine, the door slammed shut. He was alone in the room.

With a wild curse, he leaped over toward the doorway. Five feet away. Four feet—three, and he reached it and grabbed the knob. He twisted it savagely and jerked. The door refused to open, and the power of his motion pulled his hand from the knob.

He grabbed it again, twisted the other way, and jerked. The door flew open, and he found himself glaring, agate-eyed, down a long boarded passageway with another door at the far end.

The corridor was empty and silent, save for the sound of his own hoarse breathing.

CHAPTER 11
THE GREEN THUNDERBOLT

LIKE A frozen image, Dusty stood there, scanning the passageway. It was dimly lighted, and for a moment he saw only the aperture at the far end. Then with a start, he saw a large double door, about halfway down on the right.

Instantly he surmised that that was where Fire-Eyes must have entered. The great man couldn't possibly have reached the door at the far end of the corridor in such a short time. Even his stride would not warrant that.

Dusty started moving down the hallway. Gun held straight out in front of him, he went stealthily forward, like a killer jaguar stalking its prey. His determination to kill was doubled in intensity, now. Be damned to anything else. Maybe Curly and young Horner got through. Maybe they didn't. Maybe he was leaving the hill El Jatate secret behind him. Maybe he wasn't. The hell with all that—Fire-Eyes was going to die.

But as he reached the door and pressed his ear against it he heard not a single sound. He scowled a moment, then sucked in his breath with grim determination. Sticking the gun in his shirt front he wedged his fingers in the crack where the sliding doors met and silently moved them apart.

Eyes glued to the crack, he stared through, and at first saw nothing but pitch darkness. A moment later, though, he glimpsed a faint line of light. It came from under another door some twenty-five or thirty feet directly ahead of Dusty. And, as he strained his ears, he heard the sound of rasping voices beyond.

Wedging the door open wider, he squeezed himself through and slid it shut. He found himself on a wooden ramp that slanted down toward the light. As he eased silently down the ramp, his groping hands touched metal drums. A thrill shot through him. He was touching drums of liquid Tetalyne.

A sudden urge to search the room possessed him. But the muffled booming of Fire-Eyes' voice kept him to his original course. Like a cat, he sneaked forward the rest of the way and reached the door. It was then that he saw it was open a crack. Heart thumping madly, he peered through. And what he saw made his blood run cold.

He was looking at a high-domed room. It was large and

undoubtedly circular, though the door cut off part of it. But it was what was in the room that momentarily stunned him.

Slanting up from the center of the floor was a large grooved tube that extended through the domed ceiling at approximately a thirty degree angle. The tube was about seven feet in diameter and heavily braced to the floor.

At its lower and open end, resting on a slanting platform, much the same as a shell and powder loading platform for a naval gun, was an object that took his breath away completely. Never in all of his life had he seen quite anything like it. His first impression was that he was looking at a tear-drop-shaped fuselage without wings. On the pointed nose was a metal propeller. And at the tail were four large fins set at right angles to each other. The lower part of each fin extended forward clear to the nose. And as he stared at them he realized that they were constructed to fit into the flange grooves in the giant tube that slanted upward.

Between each fin were split exhaust pipes. Fitted to the fins themselves were gas rocket cells. The rear end of the strange craft was a bumper head that rested flush against the driving head of a large electro-hydraulic piston. The entire craft was about twenty-five feet long, a good six feet thick at the thickest point and was painted a brilliant green.

Instantly he thought of the green sections of dural he'd seen in the other room. And the answers to a lot of questions that had been tormenting him, sliced into his brain. The thing was a combination rocket plane and shell. Though that was just guess work on his part, he was sure that he was right. There was the answer to what had happened at Dayton and Test Field 12 and Texas-Four. There was the reason for all those drums of Tetalyne and rocket gas. There was—

HE DIDN'T finish the rest of the silently stated conviction. His eyes had seen something else—something that made his blood boil. Off to his left and standing with their backs to him were Fire-Eyes and the Hawk. And in front of them, bound helpless in a chair, was Agent 10. The man's face was white and wane looking, but savage defiance burned in his eyes.

Jack's presence explained why the two Blacks had gone tearing out of that machine shop. The third man had come to say that young Horner had been captured.

"The devil with your language. I'll speak only American!"

Agent 10's words made Dusty realize that the three had not been speaking English. Then he heard the Hawk.

"Very well, I ask you in English—where are those two friends of yours? Did they both get away in that plane?"

Dusty's heart leaped. God, had Curly made it? He listened breathlessly for young Horner's answer.

"That is for you to wonder about, Hawk! I'll see you in hell before I'll tell you. And that goes for you, too, Fire-Eyes!"

There followed a moment of utter silence, and then the Black commander-in-chief moved closer to him, and bent over. Unconsciously, Dusty raised his gun, but he checked the movement. If he shot now, he might hit young Horner.

"So you wish to puzzle us?" boomed Fire-Eyes. "But, we do not wonder. We only hope that Captain Ayres did escape in his plane. It is what we planned for him to do."

FIRE-EYES MOVED CLOSER.

Dusty saw Horner start violently. Agent 10's eyes were boring into the Black's face.

"What do you mean by that crack?" he snapped. "Hope he did escape? You'd give your right arm to have that man here, right now. All right, I will tell you. He did get away! And right now he's arranging to blow you and this place off the map. What do you think about that?"

A grating laugh drowned out the last.

"I think that you are very stupid!" said Fire-Eyes. "I will explain. Shall we say, it'll be our final salute to you? Very well, visualize the northern Front. The section between Chicago and Detroit is heavily fortified on both sides. For days we have been making offensive operations, and have drawn many of your reserve units up to that point. And now, we have concentrated a major portion of your Air Force at that point, too."

"Don't make me laugh!" cut in young Horner scornfully. "There is no reason for more than a couple of units to patrol that area. I suppose you asked all the others to go up there, too?"

Dusty saw Fire-Eyes shake his head, and the man's next words went through him like a knife.

"No, fool! It was Captain Ayres who issued the emergency order for them to mobilize there tonight, and stand by for a major offensive at dawn."

"You're crazy!"

Agent 10 flung the words at the green-masked face.

"On the contrary," the other boomed back, "we are more clever than you give us credit. Did you think that we do not know Captain Ayres' official code number? Did you think that we do not know that an emergency wave-length call from his plane would be instantly picked up by all stations?

"And did you think that we do not know that your own father was waiting word from Captain Ayers? Your father ordered Captain Ayres, and his comrade, to abandon their flight down here. And Captain Ayres' refusal to obey was our good fortune."

"Exactly!" chimed in the Hawk, gloating. "It was to be my pleasure to personally kill your friend. But, I also made other plans, in case he managed to slip through my fingers. At dawn Captain Ayres will be the most despised man in your country. On his head will be the deaths of thousands, and the complete destruction of over half of your entire air force. And I am the one who will bring that about!"

THE HAWK'S voice rose at the last, and he thumped a clenched fist against his chest. Dusty saw rage tinged with doubt smolder in young Horner's eyes. Then the Intelligence man forced his bluish lips back in a scornful grin.

"Still like to shoot your face off, don't you?" he grated. "Well, answer me this, wiseman. Ayres got away about fifteen minutes ago. Before then, we were all together. Just when did he send this wonderful emergency message through?"

It was Fire-Eyes who answered.

"You are stupid indeed! I expected you to realize the implication. Of course Captain Ayres, himself, did not transmit the message. But, it was sent from his plane—on his official code number, over his wave-length.

"To make sure that there would be no doubt, the message was sent out while his ship was flying over your Texas area

131

headquarters. His craft was seen, and his message received. What is more, General Bradley, checked back with him, and agreed to mobilize the units.

"And the man who sent that message? Here, he stands before you!"

The Black commander swung up his long arm and pointed at the smirking Hawk.

In that moment Dusty remembered what the Hawk had said, as some Black pilot stunted the Flash above their heads. "Your plane has served the purpose of its capture!" So that was what the words had meant!

But the Hawk was talking again.

"There is the entire picture for you," he hissed at young Horner. "A greater achievement, by far, than what we had originally planned. And to me has been given the triumph supreme! Look, you see that?"

The man half turned and pointed a trembling hand at the green craft.

"That is what you came down here to see!" he roared. "My brain child—the realization of my most extravagant dreams. Four of them, smaller ones, have already done their work. But this—this is the most powerful of all.

"In the nose of that Strato-Rocket, as it has been named, is enough Tetalyne to blow up a fifty square mile area of ground. Very soon, I and my assistant will be shot twenty miles into the stratosphere. Twenty miles high, you hear that? And with those control fins, we shall guide the Strato-Rocket to where your air force is now concentrating. Then I shall open the Tetalyne contact valves.

"My assistant and I will jump. We will come down at a place where one of our planes will pick us up. But, the Strato-Rocket will continue to its objective. Automatic controls will take care of that. The rest, I am sure you can guess."

Ringing silence settled over the room. Dusty could almost hear his own heart beating. His mouth had gone bone dry, and his eyes were smarting. There remained no unanswered questions now. Every bit of the puzzle had dropped into place.

Then young Horner's taunting laugh rang out again.

"Swell!" he snorted. "A great idea—but you are very short-sighted. Hell, you don't know Dusty Ayres. What do you think he's going to do once he gets across the border? Sit down and wait?

"That lad will figure things out in no time. He'll countermand your fake orders, and then he'll lead a flock of bombers back here to wipe you out, before you even get started in that damn thing!"

Fire-Eyes' huge palm snaked out and smashed against Agent 10's head.

"Fool!" he thundered. "Captain Ayres will be helpless to do anything. In his plane there is but enough fuel for him to reach the border. Once there, our agents will see that he reaches no radio station.

"But it will not matter whether he does or not. The entire Chicago-Detroit area has been static-jammed. No message can get through. And when that area is blood-soaked my armies will sweep down through your country and crush it into sub-mission, once and for all!"

Dusty groaned inwardly. Curly would be nailed at the border. Even if he got through, it would be to no avail. Brooks didn't know what had happened. And even if by some miracle he found out, it would be too late then.

The air about Chicago-Detroit had been blanketed into silence. Below, thousands of lives, and millions of dollars of equipment were doomed to everlasting eternity. And when all that was over, a wedge of Black steel would be driven right through the heart of the country.

No! Dammit, a thousand times no. There was but one way to stop it. If Fire-Eyes died—

He didn't finish the thought. With his right toe he opened the door another inch. Eyes agate he leveled his gun. For one long second he held his breath and drew a steady bead on the Back of Fire-Eyes' head.

Then he pulled the trigger!

CHAPTER 12
MADMAN'S CHANCE

FRANTICALLY DUSTY pulled the trigger again and again, but nothing happened. Sweat poured off his brow as he fumbled at it. And then the truth smashed home to him. The trigger would work, but clay had jammed the loading chamber and the firing pin groove. It would take several minutes to dig the clay free with his finger-nails.

Stepping back from the door crack, he dug furiously at the damp sticky stuff. In the dome room, the Hawk was taunting Agent 10 with more self-praise. But Dusty wasn't listening. Heart thumping, he dug at the clay, and finally got the slide flanges of the loading chamber free. With renewed energy he went to work on the firing pin groove.

But suddenly instinct made him stand motionless, ears straining. Then he heard the tramp of heavy feet along the passageway beyond the double doors. They stopped directly in front of it. The doors started to slide open.

His body was already in motion. Like a cat, he leaped blindly to the right. His leg bumped against something hard, as he came down on all fours. Touch told him that it was a drum of rocket gas.

He went down flat, hugging the damp floor, and holding his breath. A shaft of light from the passageway cut through the wide aperture. Heavy boots pounded down the ramp and up to the door leading into the dome room.

Dusty guessed that the party included at least four Blacks. He wasn't sure, and he didn't dare stick his head out to look around the drums.

A moment later there was a sharp rap on the door. From beyond, the voice of Fire-Eyes boomed something in his native tongue. A grating voice very near Dusty answered in the same language. Fire-Eyes spoke again, and the door was shoved open.

"He-e-e la-a-a zo!"

The roaring Black Invader salute to Fire-Eyes echoed and re-echoed about the place. There came an answering salute from the dome room. Then feet scuffed through the doorway and it was slammed shut.

Hugging the floor for a moment, Dusty tried to figure out his next move. The one great opportunity to kill Fire-Eyes had slipped away. He silently cursed every ounce of clay dirt in the whole world. And he also cursed himself for not inspecting his gun before.

A wave of bitter defeat swept through him. The arrival of the other Blacks could mean but one thing—the time was getting close for them to release the Strato-Rocket on its horrible mission.

"You've got to do something! Hell man, everything's up to you, now!"

Body tensed, he hissed the words to himself. Then he groaned softly. Do? What in the name of God could he do? A jammed gun against at least six bloodthirsty Blacks, one of whom was the great Fire-Eyes. And a shut door between them.

With a savage gesture he dismissed the torturing thoughts. No time for that now. It was time for action—desperate action. It seemed as though he had been planning and scheming from the beginning of time. And now the bottom had dropped out of everything.

A sudden decision, and he got to his feet. He dug the last bit of clay dirt from his gun, and breathed a prayer that it would work now. He wasted a second or two to feel the bullet clip. A hard grin curled his lips back. Five shots in all, and there should be eight. Five shots, and six Blacks!

SNEAKING AROUND the Tetalyne drums, he went over

to the door once more. Gun gripped in his right hand, he curled his left about the knob and tried it. The door was not locked— it moved under his touch. Steeling himself, he pushed it open a crack.

The domed room was no longer brilliantly lighted. The whole place was bathed in a fused green glow. At first it surprised him, and then he saw that the propeller on the Strato-Rocket was slowly turning over. Yet the engine that drove it made no more than a faint, swishing purr.

The green glow was simply the reflection cast off by the strange craft. Most of the room's lights were dimmed, and what little light they shed was cast back from the craft's glossy sides.

The reason for dimming the lights, came to him a split second later. All available power was being used to draw back the driving head piston into cocked position. And as it moved slowly back, the bumper head of the craft moved with it.

What finally riveted Dusty's attention was the group of black uniformed figures below a sliding glass entrance to the craft. They were jabbering at a man just inside the entrance. He was dressed in what looked like a heavy woven rubber diving suit. He held a part metal and part glass helmet in his hands. To the glass part was attached a link pipe leading to a combination oxygen tank and parachute pack on his back. The man was the Black Hawk.

Dusty could just barely see the Black's ugly face in the dim light. The man seemed to be having a hard time hearing what was being said to him. He put a hand to his ear and moved his head from side, to side. Dusty cursed silently. The target was not worth the shot. He stood about a million to one chance of hitting. Nevertheless, he had to take that chance.

He started to toe the door open, and then stopped dead in his tracks. The Hawk was pointing at him. Pointing at him and jabbering at another Black in a strato-suit.

For a split second every muscle in the Yank's body refused to move. Then he realized that the Hawk was not pointing at him, but toward the door, and jabbering an order at his junior officer. In the same instant a wild plan took form in Dusty's brain.

He visioned the hordes of Black troops ready to smash down through the central part of the country. Thousands of killers awaiting the moment when hell would come hurling down out of the sky onto the American defenders. The full realization of the truth of this fired him with recklessness.

His plan crystallized as the Hawk's assistant, glass and metal helmet in hand, turned and walked toward the door behind which Dusty crouched.

Fire-Eyes was gone. Perhaps to the hidden drome to fly north and see the performance of his latest and most terrible weapon of destruction. But gone he was, and his satellites remained to carry out his fiendish orders. And there was yet poor old Jack Horner. He remained, too, so that he might drink his defeat to the dregs, while his captors laughed and mocked at him. Dusty could hear the Hawk hurling taunts at the helpless Intelligence man.

Like a flash, he moved back from the door and to the side. Back flat against the wall, he raised his gun and waited. Footsteps grew louder and louder. Would that Black never come through the door? Supposing he didn't close it behind him? Would the others see his attack in the dim light?

The footsteps scuffed to a halt. The door swung open and faint light filtered through: pale green light. A bulky figure moved past. Dusty saw it, and fixed his eye on the top of the shaggy-haired head. One more foot and he would strike.

Then suddenly, the figure turned toward him. Black eyes widened, and thick lips started to jerk open. In that instant Dusty brought the gun down. The dull, crunching thud was blotted out by the sound of the door clicking shut.

As he swung the gun down, Dusty swayed forward and curled his other arm about the Black. He almost tripped and went off balance as the heavy weight sagged against him. Easing the strain, he dragged the limp form over behind the Tetalyne drums, and dumped it onto the floor.

LAYING ASIDE his gun, he tugged and pulled at the fastenings on the man's thick rubber suit. It seemed to him that an hour dragged by before he found out how they came undone. A hundred times, he heard footsteps and voices coming toward him. An equal number of times his heart froze as he imagined that the door was opening again.

Then, finally, he dragged and pulled the strato-suit free of the Black's body.

But, pulling it off was child's play compared with trying to struggle into it himself. He was but halfway in when a spear of fire slid across the palm of his hand. A razor edged knife had slid out of the Black's belt sheath and he had accidentally drawn his palm across the edge of the blade.

He cursed silently and wasted precious seconds winding his Mexican handkerchief about the throbbing wound. Then with teeth clenched savagely, he hauled the rubber casing and boots over his legs, wiggled his arms into the top, and jammed his hands into the rubber gloves. Panting and gasping for breath, he leaned against the wall for support, and battled desperately with the air-tight locks.

His fingers encased in the rubber gloves felt like so many thumbs. A dozen times he got one fastening closed, only to have another one snap open. But, eventually he got the last one clamped shut, and the metal and glass helmet jammed down over his head. Locking that was simple, and he breathed a prayer of thankfulness as he twisted the locking lugs down securely.

Bending over, he groped about on the floor for his gun, found it and straightened up. His body felt hot and sweaty, but breathing was not difficult. Then, jamming the gun into the belt, he walked around the drums and over to the door. He paused before it, for just an instant.

"Maybe I'm crazy," he whispered fervently. "But give me just one break—for their sake! I've got to try it this way!"

With that, he opened the door and walked boldly inside.

No one noticed him enter. The Hawk was fumbling with instruments inside the Strato-Rocket and not looking his way. The others were gathered about the electro-hydraulic piston. Behind them, still lashed to a chair was Agent 10. His head was sunk down on his chest, in utter dejection.

With cool deliberateness, Dusty walked right over to the Intelligence man. He stopped at the back of the chair, slipped the knife from its sheath, and in one swift movement slashed through young Horner's bonds. Instantly the man stiffened, jerked up his head and looked around.

His jaw dropped in amazement, but snapped shut again as Dusty made a quick warning gesture. As he finished the gesture, the pilot whipped the gun from his belt, and pressed it into the other's hands.

In the dim light their eyes met for a fleeting moment. Agent 10 read Dusty's thought, and shook his head sharply. Words formed on his lips, but he remained silent. Dusty shrugged, pointed at the other's gun, and deliberately turned his back. He had played his last card. God grant that young Horner would be able to fight his way out.

And now—for the mad adventure, with only a knife for a weapon.

Crazy? Of course he was crazy! But only a madman's course lay open. What he'd do once he was inside that Strato-Rocket, he hadn't the faintest idea. But deep in his heart was a vow to thousands of Americans.

This green thunderbolt would never plunge down into their midst. Perhaps it would mean his own life. But he would know the satisfaction of having the Hawk go roaring down to hell with him.

For a moment as he trudged, head down, over toward the craft, fearful doubt gripped him. Why had he given Agent 10 his gun? Hell, he could easily plug the Hawk now. But that would not end the matter.

He might kill the Black, but one of the other Invaders would surely get him before he could destroy this fiendish craft.

That was the important thing—its destruction.

CHAPTER 13
THE ACE OF DEATH

D USTY WAS inside the Strato-Rocket! The last ten or fifteen seconds had been a living hell. Calmly he had climbed up the short flight of steps that led to the entrance, and lowered his body inside. He had seen the Hawk turn his head as he entered, and his heart had stood still. But the Black, who now wore his own helmet, had simply jerked a thumb aft, and turned back to his instrument board.

He dared not move forward and look out to see what young Horner was doing. He could only breath a fierce prayer that Jack had read his thoughts, and would not act until he, Dusty, was gone. After that, it was up to Jack to look to his own hide. He'd done what he could for his pal.

Slumped back in a small bucket seat, he peered hard at the interior of the craft. In the dim light objects were indistinct, but he was able to see enough to set the blood pounding through his veins.

On either side of him were rocket-gas valve handles; two rows of four on each side. From there, forward for about five feet, was nothing but the inner girder bracing of the dural framework sections; each section grooved to the next and held fast by locking lugs. The bottom part was boarded level to take the weight of the craft's occupants.

Five feet in front of him, sat the Black Hawk. To the man's left, on a small shelf fitted to the side of the craft, was a wireless key and a small receiving unit. To his right were three levers, and it was at them that Dusty stared intently.

He knew instinctively that the course of the craft was controlled by those levers. At the base of each one, which was shaped something like a universal joint, were cable wires that led down through the floor and aft. He guessed that they led to the control fins. In fact he was positive of it. There were not any other control surfaces except the fins.

But why three control levers? He had the answer almost as soon as he put it to himself. One of the fins was fixed. Two of the remaining three provided lateral control. And the third took care of climb. Downward movement of the craft was controlled by its rate of speed.

Then as memory rushed back, back to a lecture on stratosphere flying he had once attended at the Government Aeronautical Institute, and presented by one of the country's leading scientist-engineers, he realized just how and why this weird craft could navigate in the air.

Initial force was produced by the electro-hydraulic piston. Its terrific driving power shot the craft up through the takeoff tube. At the same time the gas rockets aft, added to the speed. At maximum altitude additional tractor power was supplied by the rocket engine in the nose. The craft was practically an airfoil in itself, and rotation movement was checked by the control fins.

Descent was left to gravity. Any hope of landing the craft was absolutely out of the question, due to the terrific speed necessary if the fin controls were to function. Thus its occupants were forced to leave the craft at high altitude, and float down by parachute.

Simple, and not too costly considering the results obtainable. As Dusty's eyes became accustomed to the dim light, he saw that the craft was little more than a firmly braced and sealed dural shell. Save for the rocket engine forward, and the gas-rocket cells aft, there was very little expensive equipment aboard.

Compared to what it would cost in Yank lives and equipment—

Dusty cut off that thought and fixed agate eyes on the Hawk. He noted that the man's left shoulder seemed stiff, and he thought of Curly. Too bad Curly's bullet hadn't gone a little to the right! Then the thought of Curly, and everything else left him. The Hawk was turning!

The Black paused, halfway round, reached up his right hand and slid the thick glass window closed, and twisted the locking lugs into place. Then he continued turning, and nodded to Dusty. The Yank sat motionless. Then he understood as he heard snarling Invader jabbering, and the Hawk pointed a shaking finger at the rocket-gas valves.

Still Dusty didn't move. He was dumbfounded that he could hear the other's voice through his helmet. And he was equally dumbfounded as to what he was supposed to do. He had been holding his head down so that the other might not see his face through the thick glass. But a moment later there was more snarling, and the Hawk leaned toward him. He sucked in his breath and took a wild chance. Reaching out his hands to the side he started to open the rocket-gas valves.

HE HEARD a howl of rage from the Hawk. Then a great whistling roar filled his head. He was slammed back against the seat, and he felt as though his lungs were being crushed against his backbone. Through blurred eyes, he saw the Hawk fighting frantically to save himself from crashing backward. The man was turned toward him, and behind the glass front of the helmet was a face white with rage.

Instinct told Dusty that they were in motion. Pinned to the seat he was being hurled up through a great shadowy tunnel. Movement of any sort was impossible. And all the time there was a shrill, eerie whistling sound in his head. It cut and slashed through his brain like knives of white flame. Somewhere in the back of his head he was vaguely aware that he had heard the sound before.

Then white light spilled through the glass window. White at first, then reddish, then golden and then it blended off into a darker and darker gray. Still he was crushed back in the seat. Breathing was like sucking flames into his lungs. A film of fire slowly seeped over his eyes. Everything became steeped in a red haze. A red haze that emitted a whistling noise.

But, suddenly, the whistling died down somewhat. The pressure against his chest eased up. His heart pumping blood once more seared his whole body with pain at every beat. From hot, sticky clamminess his body went chilly and frigid. The red film swept away from his eyes.

And it was then that he saw the Hawk moving toward him. The man was screaming words that he could not understand. Nevertheless, as his brain started to function once more, he guessed their meaning. The Hawk was cursing him for turning the rocket-gas valves on full it the very beginning. It must be that, for the Black was pointing a trembling finger at the valves.

Dusty's heart leaped. The show-down was at hand. In a matter of seconds the Hawk would be close enough to see his face. Then—

He let the rest slide as his eyes fell upon the automatic stuck in the Hawk's belt. Inside of him he laughed harshly, lunged to his feet and shot out his hand. At least he tried to shoot out that hand. But in the cumbersome strato-suit it was like slow motion.

His arms were lead pipes, unbearably heavy. He saw the Hawk's eyes blaze up; saw the man try to stop his forward movement and jerk back. But his movements were sluggish also, and Dusty's groping fingers clamped down over the gun.

With a mighty effort he pulled it free, and flopped back into his bucket seat.

"Merry Xmas, bum!" he husked out. "Did I start us off wrong?"

The effect on the other was electrifying. For an instant the Hawk froze rigid, then slowly he sank down into his seat. Inarticulate sounds filtered in through the glass and steel helmet to Dusty's ears. Then he heard spoken words.

"You—you—you, dog?"

The words choked off. Dusty nodded his head as much as his helmet would permit.

"Right!" he grated. "It's little Johnnie-on-the-spot. And we're both going for a little buggy ride."

"Fool!" came the hoarse words. "You—you might have killed us!"

Dusty laughed at the inane remark.

"Yeah, it was close, wasn't it?" he said. "But it's my first ride, you see. Now, listen—"

He cut off short as the Black moved a hand toward the control levers.

"Cut it!" he snapped. "Just hold steady or this thing pops."

"And we both die!" thundered the other. "We are over the heart of your cursed country now. If I do not move altitude control, we descend at once."

Dusty hesitated, shrugged.

"That'll be just too bad!" he snapped. "Just keep your hands still until I finish. Listen, mug, the party's over. You played your cards very tricky at the start. But I'm holding aces, now. I've got my eye on the altimeter and directional compass behind you, see? Well, you're going to hold her as she goes, see? Just one dizzy move, and bango! Now, swing around and go to work. I'm right behind you, and watching. Keep her as she goes—get me?"

The Hawk remained motionless. Dusty saw his cruel lips curl back in a smile.

"AND IF I refuse?" came the reply. "Then we shall both go

147

down on your country. There are big cities below us, my friend. I am willing to die if it helps my cause."

Dusty leaned forward.

"Just like that, eh?" he snapped. "A little show of nerve, after all these months. O.K., I'm telling you something, stupid. I could drop you off right now, and take a chance myself on getting this buggy up where it'll do my side a lot of good. But, it might be better to let you do the chauffeuring. You know all the angles."

The Yank held his breath as the other made no move, or answer. He was tempted to plug the rat and risk his chances of controlling the craft. But, thought of his original plan checked him. He wasn't sure that he'd get away with it. And above all he didn't want to send this thing thundering down into American ground.

No, dammit, it was scheduled to smack Black territory. Yeah, a little C.O.D. delivery of a rat back to his rotten kind. Sure, he'd crown the Hawk and bail out in time. But first—make the man take over control.

He moved the gun forward an inch or two.

"Last call, you!" he barked. "Do you keep this thing headed as she goes—or do I have to get tough?"

The other cursed savagely.

"I will do nothing, dog!"

"That way, eh?" echoed Dusty. "Well, that's what you think!"

With icy deliberation he drew a bead on the Hawk's wounded shoulder, and pulled the trigger.

The report of the gun in the small sealed compartment

deafened him. He saw the Hawk half spin around. Then he heard the man cry out with pain, as he clapped his right hand to his shoulder.

"Hurts, doesn't it?" Dusty roared at him. "Did I get the same spot Curly did? Take over control, now! And watch yourself!"

The Hawk cursed and groaned.

"Swine, swine dog!" he snarled savagely. "Swine dog, you will—"

"I'll put another right alongside the first!" Dusty cracked down on him. "Think I won't? Well, how's this?"

He started to pull the trigger again, but checked himself as the Hawk flung out a protecting hand.

"No—no, do not shoot again. I—I will do as you say! I will do it!"

"And the great hero doesn't want to die after all!" snorted Dusty. Then as he slowly got to his feet, "Right, now, swing around—easy like!"

Bracing himself with his free hand Dusty clamped the gun on the Hawk and watched him with an eagle eye as he slowly turned front and grasped the control levers and rocket engine throttle. A moment later the whistling sound increased in tone. Dusty sensed the craft nosing upward, and his eye on the altimeter confirmed it. In what seemed like split seconds the needle moved from the one hundred and twenty two thousand foot mark up to the one hundred and twenty five thousand foot peg.

As he glanced at it every second, Dusty thrilled to the fingertips, in spite of the tenseness of the occasion. One hundred and twenty-five thousand feet above the earth! Over twenty miles high! In an abstract sort of way, Major Pratt's remark floated back in memory. "If the Blacks have got anything that'll go higher than eighty-six thousand, I'll eat it!" Boy, what a tough meal this crate would make for Pratt!

A moment later Dusty's eye spotted something that made him stiffen. In front of the Hawk, and clamped to the instrument hoard was a deadly compressed air revolver. To get it he would have to lean past the Hawk's body. No soap, that. He couldn't risk anything now. But if the Hawk tried—

He cut off the thought, jabbed the Black in the back with his gun, and bent his helmeted head close.

"I see the air gun too," he grated. "We'll just let it stay where it is, see?"

The Hawk made no reply, but Dusty felt his body quiver. Flicking his eyes from the gun, Dusty looked at the directional compass. It was a combination compass and air-ground speed indicator. A bit of rapid calculation in his head resulted in the snap guess that they were over the southeastern tip of Missouri, and maintaining the terrific trajectory speed of close to one thousand miles per hour.

For a moment the thought stunned him. Hell, and he'd considered the Silver Flash III fast! Nuts, this was the way to go to town. Maybe some day, they'd put wings and landing gear on this type of craft, and then flying would be flying. An idea, that! Maybe—

HE SNAPPED off the rest. His head was getting light,

damnably light. No wonder his brain was rambling with a lot of dizzy thoughts. God, but his ears ached!

From a long way off he heard his own mumbled words.

"Something funny—something damned funny!"

He sucked in oxygen and held it in his lungs. That didn't seem to help. Someone was cutting his scalp off with a knife. Every joint in his body seemed to be clamped in a vice. He couldn't even move the gun.

Through flickering eyes he looked at the Hawk. The man sat motionless, one hand on the rocket engine throttle, the other spread-fingered on the fin control levers. He seemed to be all right.

Dammit, what was the matter? The damn suit was shrinking. That's what it was doing—shrinking and tightening around him like gigantic rubber bandages. His whole body was stiff as a board. He couldn't even breath. He—?

It was then that his eyes staring dully over the Hawk's shoulder saw the tiny valve on the front of the man's suit. The sight of it was like a great light exploding in his head. The oxygen valve for his suit, of course. The pores of his body had absorbed the air in his suit, and it was shrinking.

He must turn his valve and let more air into the suit. He must turn it now. In another few seconds he would be helpless. God, what a fool not to have realized it before. That valve was to counteract any leaks. And there was a leak in his suit, somewhere.

To move his arm was like trying to move a solid steel bar. A thousand hellish years dragged by, and every ounce of his strength was nearly spent, when finally he got his hand on the valve. But it froze there. He couldn't move it. He must—he must!

At that moment there was a violent hissing sound in his ears. His chest seemed to virtually snap outward, and his knees went suddenly loose and wobbly. Try as he might he could not keep on his feet. From a stiff board, he had suddenly turned to water.

"Swine fool, swine fool! Now, who is the clever one? Now, who is the clever one?"

The grating words cut through his brain. As though it were a wavering mirage, Dusty saw the ugly glass covered face turned toward him. The lips were snarling and the eyes were blazing with mad triumph. It was then that he dully realized that he had collapsed on the floor of the craft. He was half sitting up, and his back was wedged between two of the circular sectioned I beam bracing girders.

In his right hand, resting limply on the floor, was his gun. He stared at it thickly, his brain refusing to tell him what it was all about. In rapid succession his body changed from white heat to icy coldness and back again. Weird thoughts filtered through his whirling head.

He must have the bends. The bends that deep sea divers get when pressure changes is too fast. Yeah, he must have the bends. But that damn gun. It was in his hand—right in his hand, and the Hawk hadn't moved from his seat. Simply sat there with head turned around, cursing and screaming at him.

"So, you would triumph over me, eh? Fool, you have never been this high, no? I knew that. I knew it when you did not release the suit valve. And now—now it is the finish! *He-e-e la-a-a zo!* The finish for you and thousands of other dogs!"

"I'll get you—I'll get you yet!"

Dusty's voice echoed back to him, no more than a hoarse whisper. He glared at his gun, as though the very intensity of the glare would force his numbed muscles to function—to raise the gun and fire. But those numbed muscles refused to move. The fingers clutching the gun did not even stir.

He was conscious of the Hawk working the control levers. The whistling sound, which had been faint, died out altogether. The Black turned in the seat, and kicked out viciously with his foot. Dusty saw it meet his gun hand; saw the gun go sliding across the floor, yet he felt no pain. In fact, he didn't feel anything. A MOMENT later the staccato chatter of a wireless key came to him. He was too weak, too limp, to turn his head, but by looking out the corner of his eyes he could see the Hawk frantically thumping the key. The man's face was beet red with glowing, berserk joy. And his lips were drawn back, showing practically all of his fang teeth.

Presently, the man stopped pounding the key. For a moment he put phones to his ears, listened intently, then slapped the phones back on their hook and nodded in evident satisfaction. Then swinging off his seat, he knelt down beside Dusty.

"A pleasant journey! A most pleasant journey to the end of everything for you. I told you that we had met for the last time. And this is the last time. Ten minutes from now, and your blood will soak into the ground. No, it will be sprayed to the four winds. And then the greatest army on earth will grind your cursed country under its heel!"

The man ended with a wild and hideous laugh. Dusty glared at him. Put every atom of hate into the glare to hold his attention. For faint hope rippled through him. Feeling had come back to his body. He must have opened the chest valve! Blood was pounding through his veins. Not violently, but enough to electrify him with the realization that he had not turned the suit valve too late. If only he could hold this rat here a couple of minutes longer.

From a thousand miles away the sound of his own voice came back to him.

"Not there, yet—not there, yet it can't be!"

The Black shoved his smirking face closer.

"But we are! See—my hand touches the rocket throttle. I but pull it back, and our speed slackens. Then the craft heads down. The speed will not be great enough to keep it aloft. It goes down, down—and the control fins will hold it at the correct diving angle. Nothing can stop it!"

Dusty looked at him glassy-eyed.

"God, you wouldn't do that?" he sobbed out thickly. "I let you live—you wouldn't dare—"

A snarling scream of joy cut him off.

"Listen to him—listen to the great Captain Ayres, now. Wouldn't do that? It will be the greatest moment of my life! Goodbye, my brave captain. I open the window. And now, I pull back the throttle—"

At that instant Dusty summoned every ounce of his sluggish

THE HAWK WAS PULLING HIMSELF OUT OF THE OPENING.

strength, and flung himself over on his side, and stretched out his hand toward the gun the Hawk had kicked away. His fingers clawed into the floor two inches from it. A howl of rage smashed against his ears. Through a red blur he saw the Hawk snatch the air gun from its clamps.

The craft had tilted sharply down by the nose. Dusty felt himself rolling away from the gun. Then it came sliding down into his fingers. He clutched it, wrenched over on his back. A ton of lead was on his arm. He moved it up—up—up!

A shadow hovered above him. It was the Hawk pulling himself out of the opening. Something in the man's hand spat misty fire. A sledgehammer smashed against Dusty's right knee. There was a thunderous roar, and his own gun hand jumped. He heard a scream, and the shadow fell away from the opening.

"Up—up! Get him!"

Even before his voice roared out the words, he was clawing up toward the opening. Fire encased his whole right leg, but he hardly felt it. Cursing, shouting, sobbing wildly he clawed at the I beam girders, and pulled himself up. Somehow he managed to hook his gun arm over the edge of the opening. His left hand grabbed the side jamb. A terrific whirring sound filled his ears, and a gigantic unseen force tugged at his gun arm, and his head.

Before him, everything was a milkish blur. Then he saw a dark shape twisting over in the air in front of him and slightly below. Only when the gun leaped in his hand did he realize that he had pulled the trigger. And then suddenly, something smashed into his throat. It was a terrific blow that jerked his head back in a flash. Something seemed to snap inside his head. Colored lights spun around, and the roar of a thousand earthquakes thundered against his brain.

He was toppling over backwards. In a last desperate effort, he flung out his hands. The gun slapped against the side of the opening, and went flying off into space. And a second later he crashed down onto the floor in a heap.

CHAPTER 14
DIVING CHAOS

A S HE hit, he tried to roll over and get to his hands and knees. The fires of hell itself were in his lungs. He sucked in air and choked. His body was swelling up—it was going to explode.

Already it seemed as though his head was floating off from his shoulders. Everything became bluish white. He raised a hand to the front of his helmet. It caught on something and stuck. He looked down and saw that it was caught on a jagged piece of the link tube leading around under his arm to the oxygen tank on his back.

It was instinct and nothing else that told him what had happened. The Hawk's parting shot had drilled his oxygen link tube. And the high altitude was doing the rest. Fortunately not all of his blessed life-giving oxygen had escaped from the tank. But he had sucked in some of the rarified air, and his lungs were unable to stand it.

Even as instinct drove home that truth he curled his rubber glove about the jagged hole and squeezed with all his might. Then he drew on the tube between his teeth. Blessed relief flooded down into his lungs, and sent tingling energy to every part of his body.

Bracing himself, he staggered to his feet. The Strato-Rocket was thundering downward at unbelievable speed now. It was all he could do to hold himself up on the slanting floor. A dozen times he tried to pull himself up to the opening. But without the use of both hands it was impossible. And he didn't dare let go of the link tube.

"Level it off—the throttle—the throttle!"

His own yelling voice sent him lurching forward. He half fell into the seat, grabbed the throttle and opened it wide. Whistling sound drummed against his ears. There was a violent upward jerk of the craft that flung him over backwards.

It was then that he realized he had shoved his shoulder against the altitude control lever. Twisting in the seat he put it in neutral. And on level keel the craft streaked forward.

But it was only momentary relief to that half crazy Yank. The craft slanted down by the nose again, and before Dusty's blurred eyes the altitude needle slid around the dial like the second hand of a watch. Even as he looked at it the hand slid past graduation marks equivalent to almost forty thousand feet.

He jerked back the altitude fin lever again. The needle slowed up, but it continued to move around the dial. Cold fingers of fear and dread curled about his heart. The rocket-gas aft was ebbing fast, and there was not enough force left to keep the craft on even keel. It was going down—slowly, but going down.

The realization smashed and slammed through his head. He stared dully at the directional compass and air-ground speed indicator. Then he glanced at the angle of travel gauge and groaned aloud. As far as he could calculate the Strato-Rocket was over the southern rim of the Chicago-Detroit area and going down at a forty degree angle.

"I've got to hold it off—I've got to!"

He groaned out the words, and pulled the altitude control

lever all the way back. The needle slowed up a bit more, but the craft still slanted downward. He banged the throttle. That helped a bit. The nose came up some.

"CURLY"

A wild cry of joyous relief burst from his lips as he saw the altitude needle pause and quiver at the forty thousand foot mark. But as he took his hand away from the throttle, vibration made it slide back. And down went the nose again, and the altitude needle swung around to thirty eight thousand.

Vibration—engine vibration! The words seemed to explode in his head. The throttle would not stay wide open because of vibration. It was the pitch of the prop in heavy air that caused it. To get this hell craft beyond the American side of the area he would have to stay and hold the throttle open.

"Jump, you damn fool! Bail out while you have time. Maybe,

you won't strike them anyway! Bail out while you have the chance!"

The sound of his own frantic voice suddenly steadied his whirling brain. The spinning stopped, and cool, deliberate reasoning took charge. Yeah, he could jump now. He was still pretty high but his snagged air line would hold out until he didn't have to depend upon it. At least the chances were in his favor.

So strong did the urge flood through him, that before he realized he was moving, he had climbed up on the seat and was hooking his free arm around the edge of the opening. Yup, he could get through now. Why the hell hadn't he tried this before, instead of trying to pull himself up through? He—

At that instant his brain made a sharp cracking sound. A terrific rush of air was forcing his head back against the aft side of the opening. And he was staring down at a thin layer of ground mist far below.

One flash glance and the horrible truth struck home. His calculations had been wrong. He was only, now, directly over the southern rim of the area. He was headed straight for the heart of the American defenses. He couldn't see them clearly. Hell, he didn't have to. He knew what was below.

"Back you fool—back you yellow-belly! By God, you won't quit now!"

As he shouted the words he flung himself savagely back into the seat. Bringing up his right foot he smashed it against the rocket throttle and rammed it wide open. The altitude needle quivered at twenty five thousand, then it started sliding down—sliding down slowly.

To Dusty, it was the finger of doom—the finger of doom pointing at him. He groaned, then laughed insanely. At least he would complete the job. The diving angle was still flat enough to carry him over into Black territory. He'd reach those rats with fifteen thousand feet to spare. Then would come his chance. If he could get clear in time, and if Lady Luck stuck with him for just a few seconds after that!

And then with an impulsive movement he shot out his free hand to the wireless key. Hell, there was still Mex-Twelve! There was still Mex-Twelve to be cleaned up. A job that still remained for him to do.

With his thumb he snapped on full transmission volume, and prayed to God that he was above the static blanket that the Blacks had flung over the Chicago-Detroit area. And then he started pounding the key, his eyes glued to the altimeter needle.

Y-A-N-K B-O-M-B-E-R-S G-O T-O E-L J-A-T-A-T-E M-E-X-1-2 A-T O-N-C-E E-M-E-R-G-E-N-C-Y A-Y-R-E-S.

Over and over again he pounded out the message in International Morse. His fingers ached and went numb, but with teeth clenched he pounded the key frantically.

And then finally he stopped. The altitude needle was passing the sixteen thousand foot mark. Now, was the greatest moment of all.

"A break, oh God for just one break!"

The shouted prayer rushed from his lips as he scrambled up onto the seat. Instantly the nose started to drop. His outflung arms missed the opening, and he fell away. Twisting and squirming, virtually in mid-air, he somehow managed to hook a hand over the edge. He felt that it was being ripped off at the shoulder.

In a lunging motion, he got his other arm through. Then his helmet banged against the top of the opening. A terrific rush of air caught his head and shoulders. Through a bluish grey haze he saw earth far below him. For a flash instant he recognized landmarks, and berserk joy swept through him.

He was directly over the heart of the Black defenses, and dropping straight down, like a meteor from another world!

And then everything merged into a great whirling conglomeration of shadows. Something jerked his body out and away. A flash of green whipped past him, and in the next instant he was spinning through space like a human pin-wheel.

But a moment later he was flat on his back on a beautiful white cloud. No, as his eyes cleared he realized dully that the beautiful white cloud was directly above him. And it was swinging him around in the air at the end of taut cords.

Then, and then only, did his foggy senses register the fact that he had pulled his parachute release ring.

"Made it! Damned if I didn't. How's that for—"

He never finished the rest.

At that moment earth and sky exploded in one thunderous roar of sound. It seemed to drive the base of his skull up into his brain. A billowing mass of crimson leaped up and engulfed him. He was hurtling straight through the very center of hell. Everything was glowing crimson—glowing crimson that roared out horrible crashing sound.

Up, up, up he went. Then some unseen force smashed into him, and he went curving outward and down. Then up he soared again, like a tiny cork caught in the swirling waters of a raging sea. His arms and legs were being pulled free from his body. From head to foot piercing, excruciating pain slashed and sliced through him.

And then, like the snapping off of a light switch, his senses stopped registering pain. Yet, his brain still functioned—functioned spasmodically. His body was dead, but his brain still lived on. He could see the lower part of his body swinging down through a red, smoking hell. He could even see the silk folds of his parachute.

Now it was above him, and now he was above it. The silk flapped and snapped. He even saw a small rip in the very center. The rip grew larger and larger. Then he lost it to view, as his body was twisted about.

Suddenly, the red hell floated away from him. There was a brownish blur below, and something that shimmered far off to his right. Brownish blur? All unconscious to him his brain toyed with the question. Brownish blur—brownish blur! Bro—the ground!

The last shot through his brain, but to his dulled senses it didn't mean anything.

An instant later, clawing fingers raked him from head to

163

foot. His suit was ripped open in a hundred different places. And then something crashed into the small of his back. Air whistled out of his lungs, and his whole chest seemed to cave in on top of his heart. But all motion had ceased. He was no longer floating or falling. He was still—absolutely still, and blurred grey fingers were weaving about before his eyes.

"The finish, huh? The finish! Never pictured it like that. Damn fingers—grabbing me, grabbing me for the finish!"

Then for a fleeting moment clear vision came to his eyes. He was on his hands and knees staring through the branches of some bushes. Beyond them shadows were racing toward him. Without knowing it, he struggled to his feet. The shadows changed into figures of men—figures of soldiers running toward him with leveled rifles. Figures of soldiers—

"Yanks!" The word burst from his throat. "Yanks!" he bellowed. "Bombers to El Jatate Mex-Twelve—Bombers to Mex-Twelve— El Jatate—bombers—!"

"Steady, lad, steady! It's all right, now. Just take it easy and relax! Here, just a sip."

Liquid fire sliding down his throat drew aside a curtain from Dusty's eyes. He saw faces, familiar faces. One was that of Curly Brooks. Another of General Horner. Another of General Bradley. And the fourth—Jack Horner!

He closed his eyes, then opened them again. The faces were still there. Behind them was the bleak white wall of a military hospital ward. He tried to look to the side, and discovered that he could not even move—not even his hands.

"Steady lad! It's all O.K. now."

Curly Brooks' lips were moving, yet to Dusty's ringing ears the words seemed to come from all directions. He moved his tongue; it filled his whole mouth.

"Who—what—how the hell did I get here? God—Mex-Twelve, you fools! Bombers must—"

General Horner's hand reached out in a silencing gesture.

"Mex-Twelve has been all taken care of, son," the senior officer said gently. "And thanks to you, we were able to drive the Blacks clear out of the Chicago-Detroit area—back to the Canadian line. Now you just rest and get some more sleep."

Dusty stared at him blankly, as memory began to filter back to him.

"Drove them back?" he grunted. "Hell—just blew up the place a few minutes ago. But how'd I get here so quick?"

Curly moved closer and grinned down at him.

"Papa says for sonny boy to shut up! We'll do the talking. You blew up that area over a week ago. But ever since our ground troops lugged you in—you came down just inside the outpost line—you've been raving your head off about all that happened. As the general said, Mex-Twelve is all in small pieces. Your real emergency call got through. The wireless one I mean. And our bombers did the job that very same day."

Dusty frowned.

"And they didn't get you, kid?"

Curly laughed.

"Nope. Had a little trouble at the border, but I just borrowed some of your luck, and wiggled away. As a matter of fact, just in time to join in on the tail end of the bombing show."

Dusty wasn't listening to the last. His eyes were clamped on Jack Horner's pale face.

"Did you get him, by any chance, Jack?"

The Intelligence man's eyebrows went up.

"Huh? Who? Oh, Fire-Eyes? No, Dusty, he'd gone. But, say, something happened as that Strato-Rocket left! A cloud of flame gas caught those Blacks cold. They turned to crisps. I'd edged back, and it missed me. God, kid—if it hadn't been for you.

"Well, anyway, in the mix-up I made my exit. Hunted for him, but no soap. Some of that luck Curly was talking about came my way, and I was clear of the place when the bombers arrived. Funny though, about what happened as that Strato-Rocket took off."

"Tell you about that later," grunted Dusty, and turned his eyes toward General Horner.

The senior officer scowled.

"No more questions, Ayres!" he said. "It's only by the grace of God and a crazy man's luck that you're alive now."

"Have to ask this one," said Dusty. "I'll sleep better. That rat at Test Field Twelve was the radio officer wasn't he? You caught him, and then sent me that return order?"

The Intelligence chief continued to scowl, then nodded abruptly.

"Yes," he said. "No wonder we were tripped up on everything. That devil had planted himself in a key position. Pratt caught him later, radioing a Black station. Shot him through the head.

By the way, Pratt was not at Test Twelve when it was blown up."

"Luck all around," murmured Dusty sleepily. "Wonder if the Hawk had some, too. By the way, general, any time Major Pratt's new X-Rayoscope is ready for testing, just let me know. Sounds like a swell idea to me."

"I'm giving you an order, Captain Ayres!" said General Horner sternly. "No more questions, and no more talk! You are to get all the—"

He stopped short and grunted. Captain Dusty Ayres had already obeyed his order.

POPULAR PUBLICATIONS
HERO PULPS

LOOK FOR MORE SOON!

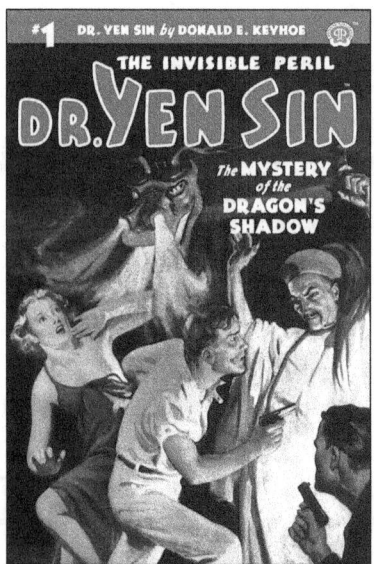

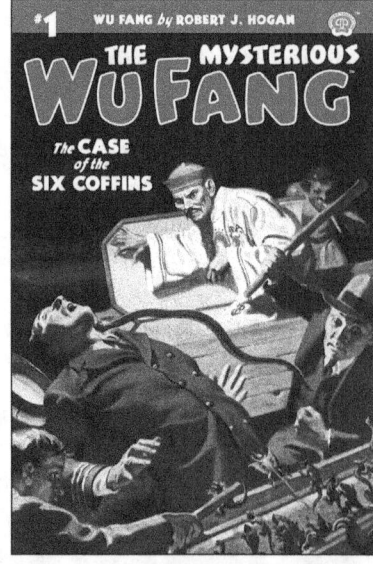